BOOKS BY CHARLES SIMMONS

Powdered Eggs
An Old-Fashioned Darling
Wrinkles

Wrinkles

Wrinkles

Charles Simmons

Farrar, Straus and Giroux

NEW YORK

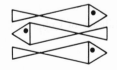

Published simultaneously in Canada by
McGraw-Hill Ryerson Ltd., Toronto

Printed in the United States of America

Designed by Guy Fleming

FIRST EDITION, 1978

Portions of this book appeared, in somewhat
different form, in American Review 24

Library of Congress Cataloging in Publication Data
Simmons, Charles.
Wrinkles.
I. Title.
PZ4.S5925Wr [PS3569.I4729] 813'.5'4 78–9269

To Nancy

Wrinkles

His MOTHER taught him numbers before he went to school. First he learned the words, which he said as he unfolded, one by one, the fingers of his fists. He had different feelings about each digit. One was perfect and friendly. Its appearance resembled its meaning. Two looked more complicated than it was. At least if he drew it schematically, like a Z, and considered the middle line as a way to get from the top to the bottom lines it also resembled its meaning. Three was pleasing: its three points made it easy to understand and remember. He could add two threes by counting their six points. Four if he wrote it with an open top had four points. The system broke down with five, and five was hard to draw; but, since it was half of ten, quick and accurate things could be done with it. Six, although it was even, resembled an odd number because it was curved like three and five. Seven was the most difficult digit; it was hard to picture the number of units it represented: the best he could do was five units and two units next to them; it was deceptively simple to draw and somehow not to be trusted. He found eight appealing because it was paradoxical: it had the curves of an odd number, but because it was vertically symmetrical it was an appropriate symbol for an even number. The only way to deal with nine was as one less than ten, and, considering how high the digit was, he did well with it: two tens were twenty; therefore two nines were two ones less than twenty, or eighteen. This worked all the way up to nine nines: that is, nine nines were nine ones less than nine tens, or eighty-one. Zero, like one, was perfect. One day when he was five and confined to bed with a cold he recognized that the series zero to nine paralleled the series ten to nineteen, twenty to twenty-nine, and so on. He felt a great surge of power and wrote on a sheet of paper the numbers one to one hundred and fifty-one. Given time he knew he could continue creating numbers indefinitely. His mother checked the list for accuracy and showed it to his father that evening. His father was pleased and said that arithmetic had been his best subject in grammar school. Since his father had not gone beyond grammar school and since, as his mother said, his father was an extremely intelligent man numbers must be a large part of his father's intelligence. Arithmetic became his own best subject in grammar school. His second-grade teacher announced at the beginning of the year that henceforth four was to be made with an open top. This suited him, but it disconcerted the other students; they had all been taught in the first grade to make four with a closed top. The thinking now was otherwise. He pictured a convention of grownups coming to this conclusion, probably during the previous summer. Because he had discovered the decimal system for himself he knew the relationships expressed in the multiplication tables, but the teachers insisted that he and the other students learn the tables by rote. As a result, when asked to multiply, he ran through the memorized tables and in time lost his feel for numerical architecture. In the first year of high school he was taught elementary algebra by a buck-toothed eccentric; the admixture of letters diluted the elegance of numbers, and mathematics became his poorest subject. By the time he had entered the army he had forgotten parts of the multiplication tables—six times seven, seven times eight, eight times twelve—and he did poorly on the army intelligence test. He went to his commanding officer, explained the problem, and asked to be retested. The night before the test, he wrote down the tables, working out some of them by addition, and committed them to memory again. Now his interest in numbers, beyond such practical uses as figuring household budgets and checking bank balances, is mystical. He is struck by the recurrence of mid-eighties and mid–eight hundreds in his life. His house number when he was a child was eight-forty; his high school was on Eighty-fourth Street; he got off at the Eighty-sixth Street subway station to visit his first serious girl friend; when the Dow Jones average of industrial stocks is in the mid–eight hundreds he feels he should buy or sell. He will buy an electronic calculator and play with it in periods of stress. The effortless answers it provides to arithmetic problems within its scope will relax him as watching sports had when he was younger. One day when he is haphazardly drawing square roots from the calculator and squaring them to determine the inadequacy of decimal approximations he will realize that from childhood he had unconsciously thought he could be and then could have been a mathematician, and he will now realize that he could not. This will be a relief to him. In his sixties he will wonder if the recurrence of numbers in the mid-eighties in his history will apply to the end of his life.

His Aunt Mae lived with them off and on through his childhood. She had been the oldest child in his mother's family; his mother had been the youngest. His friends said that Mae seemed more like a grandmother than an aunt. She was thin, had gray-blond hair, fine features, and a wary look. She paid greater attention to him than to his brother and on Saturday afternoons took him wherever he wanted to go. She had done many things for a living; she was proud of having worked at exclusive seaside New Jersey hotels, in what capacity he didn't know. When she stayed with his family she earned money addressing envelopes; she had a good hand and would sit at a table by a window with a pile of envelopes and a list of names and addresses and work for hours without fatigue or complaint. Her pen had a gold loop on the cap, and she wrote with a perforated red rubber guard on her index finger. She wouldn't let anyone use her pen: "It might disturb the set of the nib." She had been married to a Texas widower who had worked as a hotel manager and river boat captain and had finally settled down on a Florida orange grove. After the marriage broke up she retained the man's name and occasionally told mildly heroic stories about him: once in Florida she found on the kitchen table a tarantula "ready to spring"; she called to her husband, who said not to move, appeared with a wet towel, and snapped the thing dead. He asked her why she had left her husband. Because he kept a loaded pistol on the night table, she said. He asked his mother the same question about Mae; she said that Mae liked to travel, enjoyed hotels and river boats but not the orange grove. When he got bigger he could do by himself the things he had done with Mae; still they stayed close. She agreed with his points of view, even when, he felt, she didn't understand them and even when they contradicted those of his father and brother (except when his father or brother was present). She answered questions generously, and since she had been many places she knew many things. However, he doubted some of what she said: she claimed that appendicitis was caused by swallowing apple seeds; food that took long to cook, like candy, was cheaper to buy in a store because of the price of gas; after a certain age one shouldn't walk barefoot in the sand because the grains worked through the pores into the blood stream. Mae took up little room and had few possessions. She owned one book, *The Standard Cyclopedia of Recipes* (by F. E. Brown, copyright 1910), which contained 1,001 recipes: how to stiffen hats, soften corsets, make imitation brandy, cure cancer (there were five cures for cancer, two of them "sure"). She would let him have the book for short periods but got anxious if it was out of her hands for long. When he was about to be married he told Mae and his mother that his fiancée had insisted he go to confession so that he could receive Communion at a nuptial mass, and he had lied to her about the going to confession. He thought it was an amusing story; however, Mae in a loud voice, which he had not heard before, accused him of self-indulgence and double-dealing—"and you've always been like that, since you were a baby," she said. He and his mother were taken aback: they thought Mae had been fond of him. He and Mae were then cool to one another, even after his mother reported that Mae was sorry for what she had said. When his father died he was glad Mae was around to keep his mother company. In her eighties Mae curled up on one of his mother's couches, didn't move, refused a doctor, ate little, voided little, lost weight. He put her into a hospital, intending that after a checkup she would be transferred to a home. In the hospital it was clear that she was dying. She was so frail no one was eager to find out what was wrong with her beyond the fact that there was a "sizable mass in the abdominal region." A nurse consoled his mother with the information that Mae was "not in pain," from which he gained a sense of how bad some deaths could be. No one came to the funeral home besides his mother, his brother, and himself. When his mother is the only survivor of her original family he will ask questions about the past, and often she will say, "Mae would have known that." "It may be hard to believe," she will tell him, "but Mae was a very attractive young woman, lots of men were interested in her." He will understand that his mother feels more fortunate than Mae because she has had a proper marriage and children. Near the end of her life she will say, "I'm glad Mae went first so she didn't have to be alone," from which he will conclude that she knew that neither he nor his brother would have attended Mae. "I always felt sorry for Mae," she will also say, "she was the oldest and got the worst of it." "And you were the youngest and got the best?" he will say. She will nod and smile.

His eight years at St. Ursula's Grammar School coincided with the depression. Families could not afford to move from one neighborhood to another so that the student body stayed the same. The first grade was taught by Miss Thoma, who was pretty and young and told him that he always arrived at school with a smile. The second grade was taught by Miss King, whose breast once fell out of her brassière when she was picking up chalk from the floor; she turned to the blackboard to put the breast back. The third grade was taught by Sister Noelita, whom everyone liked—boys and girls, bright and stupid, docile and sassy. One day she brought to class her twin brother, who was amusing and played the guitar. The class asked her to bring him back. She said she would, but he never came. The fourth grade was taught by Mother Ecclesiastica, the oldest nun in the school. She was brown and wrinkled and once whipped him and another boy with a cat-o'-nine-tails after ordering them to bare their calves by dropping their socks from the bottoms of their knickerbockers. His mother went with him to school the next day, complained to the principal, and there were no more beatings, not even with a ruler. Sister Noelita, again, taught the fifth grade; everyone thought this was great good luck. She left the order the next year, just before she was to make her final vows. One of his classmates said he would marry her someday. In the sixth grade, boys and girls, who had studied together, were separated. The boys' class was taught by Sister Barnabas, a tall handsome woman who said she preferred teaching girls. The seventh grade was taught by Sister Clement, a pleasant and sensible woman whose skirts he and some other boys tried to look up, through the grated landing of the rear exit, from which she oversaw play at recess. Sister Clement gave him the biography of a Catholic youth, dead twenty years, blessèd but not canonized. She said the youth reminded her of him. He did not read the book; the idea of it made him feel like a fraud. The eighth grade was taught by Sister Immaculata, who held that modern inventions and discoveries other than medical ones were bad. For instance, radio waves made street noises carry farther, and therefore teaching was more difficult. She also claimed that the classroom floors were getting harder year by year. She told how her uncle, an independently wealthy man, had developed from herbs a cure for cancer. However, he had taken the secret with him to the grave. "May God forgive him," she said. Following on the cue, one boy asked whether her uncle's refusal to share his discovery with mankind was a mortal sin. Her eyes glistened with tears as she said that it was not for her to judge. A couple, friends of Sister Immaculata, asked her to take their son into her class; the boy had been expelled from a number of schools. She explained to the class that this boy came from a privileged background and was spoiled. The boy had a big head. The class rallied against the boy, and after three months the boy was put on trial. Sister Immaculata appointed a prosecuting attorney, a defense attorney, and the jury; she was the judge. After two days of argument, the boy was found guilty of being a cheat, a coward, and a bully. In passing sentence, Sister Immaculata said that the trial had been punishment enough, that the boy had obviously been taught a lesson, and that she hoped he would turn over a new leaf. The church organist was a frail, slow-gaited, gray-haired man who was said to have once been a religious. The organist and his wife had an idiot son, who stumbled and slavered. Sister Immaculata confided to the class that the boy may have been God's punishment for past sins of one or both of the parents. Every now and then he drives past the church and school, always at night. Like so many landmarks of his childhood, these seem to have become smaller. The once German and Irish neighborhood is black and brown. By happenstance one of the older boys in a family from his early summer community is pastor now. He hears from friends that this priest is bitter at having been assigned to a poor parish. The local candy store and the garages that served the nearby middle-class Jewish population remain. In a few years he will, on impulse, take a newspaper ad calling for a reunion of his classmates. Three, all male, will come to a downtown restaurant—a police lieutenant, the manager of a hardware store, and an unemployed former boxer and stagehand. He will learn that the brightest boy of the class was an executive in a Maryland engineering firm and is now dead, that the boys who ranked second and third at graduation are also dead. He will wonder if there is meaning in this, since he was fourth.

His mother was a practicing Catholic, his father a nominal Protestant; as a result he was brought up Catholic and religion was not discussed at home. His mother taught him to say prayers but only as a ritual. The world seemed to work without God's intervention, and although he did not depend on God he occasionally called on Him to avoid danger or discomfort. If, say, on going to bed he thought he might wake in the night and be sick to his stomach he would ask God to keep it from happening. Or he might ask his mother to agree to give him ten cents next morning if it did. Either measure helped him go to sleep. He had no problem with the idea of God until he went to school and nuns raised theoretical questions about dogma as if to answer them before they occurred to the students.

If God knows all things, a nun said, does He know what we will do? The students all said yes. How can we have free will, then, the nun said, since if God knows what we will do before we do it we can't do anything else? No one could answer the question, and he found that the nun's explanation was like a magician's trick: he knew it was an illusion but couldn't figure it out. How can it be, the nun said, if God is all good, there is so much evil in the world? The answer— that man brought it on himself through the misuse of free will—was not satisfactory. Why did God give man free will if God knew man would misuse it? he asked the nun, adding that *he* would not have. But you are not God, the nun said, as if this were an explanation. He invented other questions for the nuns: Two infants are being taken to the church to be baptized; one dies on the way, the other on the way back; the second goes to heaven, the first does not. How could an all-just God have arranged things that way? When pressed like this the nuns would say the matter was a Mystery; one nun used the word *Mystère,* explaining that it was French for certain profound and beautiful turning points in theology. He and the other students were required to spend many hours in church; the ceremonies bored him, as did the prayers and hymns. To amuse himself he studied the profiles, half-profiles, and backs of heads of the girl students, who sat together on the opposite side of the church. By long practice during masses he trained himself to separate the fingers of his right hand alternately two-and-two, then one-two-one; he also mastered the exercise with his left hand, and eventually could perform one separation with one hand while performing the other separation with the other hand. None of his friends could duplicate the feat. On the black leather cover of his prayer book stamped in gold were the words *GOD'S CHILD*. The *D* in *CHILD* was worn away, and sometimes he entertained the thought that the *D* had been an *L,* thus implying that God was afraid of him and he was a rebel on the order of Lucifer but more dangerous. In condemning sin the nuns pointed out that sin was contrary to Natural Law— that is, bad in itself; an even greater reason for avoiding sin, they said, was that sin made God suffer. He found this difficult to understand: if God was all-powerful, all-knowing, etc., presumably God was happy, or should be. If *he* were God, he reasoned, he either wouldn't let sin bother him or would make men virtuous. He continued to raise objections in high school, so that one of the Jesuit priests proposed that they meet twice a week to discuss faith and morals. After four months of meetings he struck on an argument against faith that the priest could not refute: it was agreed that to commit mortal sin it was necessary to believe in mortal sin, so that from the point of view of making

God suffer he was less offensive than most believers and the priest should not try to change his convictions. The priest discontinued the interviews but asked him to say one Hail Mary a day, promising that if he did "grace would come." He promised that he would, but he didn't. When he was first married he argued with his wife against the existence of God. Neither convinced the other. Eventually she came to agree with him, but by then he didn't care about her beliefs. In his thirties when he thought he was going to die, he addressed himself to Jesus: I want your help, he said; I don't want to have anything to do with priests; you and I know about priests. He wonders now whether in fear of death he again would pray and hopes he would because it would be a comfort. He is drawn to politicians who claim to believe in God because he has come to think that the historical excesses of the century could not have been committed in a religious time. He will be drinking in a bar with a friend, who has revealed to him many intimate autobiographical details. On impulse he will ask if the friend believes in the divinity of Jesus. The friend will say, "I don't know you well enough to answer that," from which he will infer that the friend does. As he watches contemporaries die he will see that nuns make the best nurses.

WHEN HE WAS two years old he moved to a new apartment house. He liked the new house, but he did not like leaving the old one. The new apartment house had twelve entrances, all facing a garden. In the center of the garden, under an arched bridge, was a pond. Goldfish swam there in the summer; in winter the pond was drained. He and his friends wondered where the goldfish were kept in the winter. Across the street from the front of the building, to the west, stood the Boy Scout Hall, a small wooden house on top of a hill, under a large tree. To the south was a large yellow-brick building in which yeast company chemists did experiments, also an empty lot where boys played baseball, played football, sledded, or made fires, according to the season. To the east and rear was a train yard. And on the north was a rocky plateau where long weeds grew that could be pulled up and used as spears and where the ground broke into dry clumps that could be thrown or dropped and would burst on impact into clouds of dust. The window of his room opened onto the junior playground, which was filled with sand. The sand in the shady part stayed damp; with it he and his friends made runways for toy autos. When he was kept in for being bad or sick he talked to his friends from the window. Boys of ten and older could use the senior playground, on the opposite side of the building. It was made of brick and concrete and was good for playing handball, punchball, stickball, and catch. The windows of one of the stores in the rear of the building were painted dark green to a point above the eye. This store was the Men's Club, where men in the building played pool and cards. Members had to be twenty-one. His father played cards there one night a week and discussed the game with his mother at dinner the next evening. The building had many cellars. These were used for storing furniture, carriages, and sleds, and for housing dumb-waiters, boilers, and coal. Over the years he and his friends had obtained keys to the cellars and explored all of them but one, the deepest, reaching far under the garden. Lighting no matches for fear of being seen by Fred, the lantern-jawed German janitor who lived there, they worked their way along the rough walls. When they could go no farther they lit a match. Hundreds of water bugs, big as toys, scurried to and fro over the black floor. The boys bruised themselves in their panic to get out and never went back. When he was seven his family moved to a larger apartment in the building so he and his brother could have separate rooms. He did not like sleeping alone and losing his view of the playground. Now his window opened onto the train yard, and at night the light from the switched tracks flashed on his ceiling. When he was thirteen his family moved again, to another building four blocks away. He went back every Sunday to the old house to visit a friend, thinking his parents thought he was in church. Later his mother told him they knew he was visiting the friend. Now that he was no longer a resident he realized he would never be a member of the Men's Club. Actually he went into the army when he was eighteen, and by the time he got out he had no use for clubs or all-male companionship. Also, because of the postwar business boom the clubroom was rented to a dry cleaner. Other changes occurred over the years. The Boy Scout Hall burned down, the hill on which it had stood was dug away, and a great white courthouse was erected. The yeast company moved out of the city, and a ten-story apartment house, the highest in the neighborhood, appeared on the site. The same sort of thing happened to the rocky plateau. The train yard remains, but before long the air space above it will be sold and a twenty-three-story apartment house will be built and will be called "Skyline Spires." Although he will return by chance and intention every now and then he will not realize how shabby the building has become until one autumn evening when, in his fifties, he will stroll into the garden and on the bridge begin to chat with the night watchman. He will see the boy in the face of the watchman, who is about his own age, and will ask the watchman if by chance the watchman grew up in the neighborhood. No, the watchman will say, he comes from Pennsylvania. And, yes, the place has changed. "There's a different element here now," the watchman will say. Garbage in the halls. A murder two months before. "People like yourself come in here and talk about how it used to be." Did the watchman know the names of any of these people? "No, but it must have been a nice place. There's a different element here now." The slate paths through the garden, for no reason that he can imagine, will have been cemented over. The building will be standing when he dies, but only because the neighborhood will have fallen into decline.

His PARENTS bought a summer place in the spring of 1929 for $1,700. He was five that summer and cut his foot badly on broken glass. Three years later his parents could have bought or might have sold the place for $250. Because of the depression half of the thirty-two bungalows on the block remained empty through the thirties. He and his friends had access, with skeleton keys or through broken windows, to the unoccupied bungalows, most of which had a special character. Number seven, for instance, was sexy because one of the girls on the block was said to have undressed there for a boy from another block. Number one was haunted because its trim was black; it was visited only in daylight. Thirteen was fit for abuse because a once-flung apple adhered, dried and discolored, summer after summer, to one of its plasterboard walls; when he and his friends wanted to break something man-made they went to thirteen. As war approached and the depression eased, all the bungalows were finally sold. Thirteen was last, and it went to a childless undertaker and his wife. Jews and cars were not allowed in the community. Cars from the city were parked in lots outside, and Jews inquiring about bungalows were told they wouldn't be happy there. A majority of the inhabitants were Catholic, the rest Protestant, except for a small percentage said to be crypto-Jews. He tried to determine who these might be but could not decide on anyone for sure. The father of a girl he went with one summer was said to be a Jew, but converted; and the father did in fact seem to resemble his father's colleagues, most of whom were Jews. The swimming was excellent, particularly in his early years, when pools and sand bars formed at low tide. One boy broke his neck diving into a deep-looking pool. Sometimes he scraped his nose diving off a sand bar. Once, before he could swim, he floated on a tube out beyond his depth, and the tube lost air. It was early in the morning, before the mothers had come to the beach. The only person there was an older girl from the block; she swam out to save him. In his panic he pushed his palms against her breasts and understood for the first time that breasts did not have bones. (Years later he heard that she had developed breast cancer and wondered if there was a connection.) His day started with orange juice brought to him in bed by his mother. Afterward he rose, washed, dressed, had breakfast of a boiled egg and bacon strip, and went to the general store to shop for his mother. Then he was free for the rest of the day. He would join one or more of his friends; they would swim, play games, or undertake adventures. They would walk, say, the two miles to the end of the community called the Point, where they would find such ocean refuse as shark carcasses; tangles of fishhooks, sinkers, seaweed, and line; blood-streaked jellyfish; exotic shells. Sometimes they would walk to the other end, which abutted a coast artillery camp, sneak inside, and examine the sixteen-inch guns, which had been there facing the sea since the World War. When he and his friends were hot from the sun and had had enough of the water they would sit in the shade of a bungalow and play word games. After lunch they would wait the hour prescribed by their mothers, swim, and begin again. Once a year they would go to a nearby amusement park and add the next more daring ride to their repertoires. One new girl in the community went on all the rides on her first trip and earned a reputation for bravery; during the war she served as a woman Marine. When he went away to the service his parents sold the bungalow. He goes back there now and then for old times' sake. (He once took his children along so they could see a favorite place of his childhood. They didn't like it.) A great stone jetty has been built at the Point to protect the waterfront bungalows from erosion. The beach has deepened; the quick fall of the shore is gone; the receding ocean, instead of cleaning the beach each winter, leaves summer debris. People drive cars directly to their bungalows, although there are still no Jews. The faces look suspicious now. He recognizes no one and feels as he walks down his own block that the inhabitants think he is a Jew. There will be apartment houses soon, built on great concrete pilings driven into the sand, and eventually the nearby city will condemn the land for a public beach.

COTTON was friendly to him, wool was not. When he was a child the male bathing suit had a small skirt, rose in the form of an undershirt over the shoulders and under the arms, and was made of wool. The feel of wet wool drying against his body was uncomfortable, and he would have gone to his bungalow to shower and change if the custom had not been to stay on the beach after swimming. Also, if he left he might miss a clamshell-scaling contest, the construction of a gravity sand course for rubber balls, a couple necking behind a downed umbrella, or any of a number of chance pleasures of the beach. In winter, woolen trousers bothered him, and if he dribbled down the side of his leg after urinating they bothered him almost as much as a wet wool bathing suit. Since he got only one new suit of clothes a year, usually before Easter, it was important to choose a smooth weave. Occasionally he would be seduced by the manly look of a rough texture and suffer for it. One morning when he was twelve he dressed before he was completely awake and mistakenly pulled his pants over his pajama bottoms. He left both garments on for the rest of the day and wore pajama bottoms for years afterwards whenever his suits were rough. Once at a party, when he was fifteen and the other guests were older, he bunched his trouser legs around his thighs, exposing the pajamas; then he stuffed a pillow under his jacket, screwed up his face, and bounded from room to room like a mad hunchback. The act was a great hit, and because he would not explain the presence of the pajamas he got a reputation as engagingly eccentric and thereby gained full admission to the group. Something of the same thing happened in the army. The winter uniform provided a rough wool shirt, which an undershirt only partially protected him from. Out of desperation he cut the collar and cuffs from a summer cotton shirt and wore it under the wool shirt. This amused the other soldiers, and their amusement made it easier for him to hide the fact that he did not like them. After the war his father began wearing drip-dry shirts and gave him fifty white cotton shirts with French cuffs and detachable collars. The ritual of affixing cuff links and collar buttons pleased him for a while, and occasionally he would reverse the detachable collar and imitate a clergyman; but one morning on his way to work his collar rode away from the shirt, which had happened before. He went into a clothing store, bought a drip-dry shirt, and changed into it at his office. That evening he threw away all his father's shirts and collars, clean and soiled. When the laundry came back the following Saturday he threw away as well the shirts that it contained. The collar buttons, although fourteen-carat gold, he tossed from an open window. Each night he washed the drip-dry shirt and wore it the next day. Eventually it turned yellow. He abandoned it and ordered two dozen button-down cotton shirts, replacing them as they wore out. Of all his clothes he most enjoyed a checked sports jacket he bought on sale for nineteen dollars at the university shop of a stylish men's store. One day an elegantly dressed man stopped him on the street and asked where he had gotten it. He later wondered if the man was homosexual. He wore the jacket for twelve years, until the armpits rotted. As modes change he takes more pride in the old-fashioned wing-tipped style of his shoes, which he buys at sales in an expensive English shoe shop. Shoemakers comment on their quality when he has them repaired. He wears double-ply black nylon stretch socks, which seem to last forever but eventually get stiff. He will buy a modified double-breasted pinstriped suit, and it will bring him many compliments. You should wear nothing but double-breasted, he will be told; but before long he will put on weight and return to single-breasted styles and even pleated trousers. For a birthday in his late fifties he will give himself the present of replacing all his ties. He will tell his older daughter what he did, and she will be offended because a month before she gave him one of the ties he throws away. In his fifties too he will again wear pajamas at night—in the army he had lost the habit— and they will be a comfort to him, reminding him of his childhood. As his hair thins he will search for a comfortable hat, not to warm his head but to keep the longer hairs in place. No hat will be acceptable, however. In his sixties he will purchase shoes two pairs at a time. His father had done the same thing when his father was sixty, as a guarantee against death. Suits he will continue to buy singly, except on one occasion when he will buy two, a sporty herringbone ("The older the bird the brighter the plumage," he will say to the salesman) and the other dark blue.

Late one afternoon, no one around, he went into the ocean. A girl his age whom he didn't know appeared on the beach and came in beside him; she took her bathing suit down to the waist and said she would take it off altogether if he would do the same. She looked angry and mocking, and he wondered if she was crazy. He stared at her breasts, hoping that as she turned with the small waves he would see some swelling, but the breasts were flat. He wanted to see her genitals, but the thought overwhelmed him; he left and went up to his bungalow. For the rest of the summer and all through the next he looked for the girl, on the beach, in the water, in church, on his nightly walks; but he didn't see her again. Had she been a one-time visitor? was that why she had taken such a chance? When he was fourteen a minister's daughter invited him to her house for dinner; he had recently taken her to a party because a friend had said that all minister's daughters were wild. After the meal the minister and the minister's wife went out. The daughter sat him on a couch and read from a child's biology text a passage called "Wonderful Mr. Penis": how the penis, usually soft and small, voided liquid waste but at certain times swelled with blood and could be inserted into the vagina, where it emitted sperm, which fertilized an ovum. As she read he felt she wanted him to demonstrate at least some of the passage; he wanted to also, but he stared into his lap, said little, and went home as soon as the minister and the minister's wife returned. At a dance in his high school to which groups of Catholic girls had been invited he watched one girl all evening; when the dance was over he followed her into the lobby, introduced himself, and asked her to another dance a month hence. She wore a riding derby, seemed amused, said yes, and gave him her number. He learned next day from a classmate that her father was an architect and she lived an hour from the city. Telling himself that it would be too hard to pick her up and drop her off, he didn't phone her. (Years later when his marriage was failing he remembered her and wondered what it would have been like to deal with educated in-laws: whether they would have helped him overcome the mixture of subservience and contempt he felt toward older people.) In his first year of college he called the minister's daughter, who he had heard was taking courses in the college drama school. Did she remember him? Yes. Would she like to go out? Yes, although she knew, she said, why he was asking her. He stood her up. The army and navy offered separate programs to college students: the army promising only that those who joined would be exempt from the draft and would be called up together; the navy that those who joined would be sent to midshipman's school and made ensigns if they qualified, sailors if not. He and his friends joined the army program; if any of them had joined the navy program they would have been dropped from the group. "You have to be careful what you take seriously," was the principle as described by one of the group, who was himself dropped for publishing in the college magazine. After two years as a soldier he was stationed in a navy town. Naval officers seemed more fortunate even than civilians: they would survive the war and be heroes too. His dentist, who practiced on the thirty-third floor of a midtown building, one day tilted the chair forward, pointed across the street to a twenty-story building, and said, "During the depression I could have had that for back taxes. Do you know what I'd be doing now?" His mouth was full of equipment, so he raised his eyebrows; the dentist, however, just nodded. He hears many regrets from people who didn't invest in stocks, land, plays; he doesn't think more money would have improved his life, except perhaps to have saved his marriage: his wife might have valued him. When he can make love no more than once in an evening he will sometimes wonder whether, if he had not masturbated, more sex would be left to him, like bullets. During bouts of hypochondria he will regret having smoked, worried, drunk, breathed city air. When one of his books fails he will tell himself that he should have written a sequel to one that had succeeded; he will think that he should have been a playwright ("My dialogue was good," he will write to a graduate student who is doing a paper on him, "my psychologizing was . . . well, I'll leave that up to you") or a poet ("The confessional mode was popular in my middle age, it might have been my answer"). In his last illness he will be particularly sorry that he had not gone to China or seen Cape Horn, where, he had heard as a child, there were the highest waves in the world.

THE BIRTHDAY of one of his friends fell on Christmas Eve; the friend received only one set of presents, some with cards saying "Happy Birthday" and some with cards saying "Merry Christmas." His birthday came in summer, and his mother always gave a party for him, with cake, ice cream, favors, and dimes for the winners of games: picking up peanuts with one's toes, crawling with a potato in the small of one's back, pitching pennies into a floating dish. Because he chose games he was good at, every year he won over half the prizes. In two consecutive years his birthday fell on weekends, and his father attended the parties; his father doubled the prizes for the games and the second year told about a birthday party at which a man was struck by lightning while sitting at a kitchen window with a woman on his lap. The only other friend with a summer birthday also had parties, at which kissing games were played; the kissing, done privately in a bedroom, was an embarrassment for everyone. The summer he was thirteen he told his mother he didn't want a party; his friends gave him no presents that year or thereafter, although on the morning of his fourteenth birthday he found on the back porch steps a gaily wrapped package of shit. He didn't tell his parents about it, because it might worry them; nor his friends, because he thought the sender might be among them and reveal himself by mentioning it. This didn't happen. Kissing games at birthday parties in the city were fun; at one party where the kissing was public a girl named Evelyn lifted a foot like a bird when she was kissed; he tried to see if she did it when he kissed her but couldn't. She smelled good, and he asked her what perfume she used; she said none, which if true meant she was the only naturally sweet-smelling person he knew. He took her to a movie theater that had an elaborate stage show, which she liked and he didn't, whereas he had liked the movie and she hadn't; he was shocked to learn at the end of the evening that she was the older sister of the worst troublemaker in his grammar school, and he didn't take her out again. When he was seventeen it happened that one of the boys in the neighborhood was having a nineteenth birthday and going into the army the following week. A large party was planned by the boy's friends: the apartment of the married uncle of one of them was borrowed; large amounts of rye, gin, rum, and beer were bought, as well as cold cuts, bread, nuts, and potato chips; only girls with sexy reputations were invited, the purpose being to get the boy who was going into the army and anyone else laid. As far as he knew, no one was; but one of the boys sent a friend who was away and had missed the party an imaginary description, in which all the boys were laid, some three times by different girls. He was supposed to have "fucked Joyce and Judy with the same rubber, which broke in Judy." The mother of the boy who received the letter found it, phoned the parents of everyone mentioned, and read the pertinent parts. His mother told him that she had received *her* call and that the woman was unbalanced. His twentieth birthday was spent traveling by train from one southern army camp to another. He celebrated his twenty-first at the Last Chance Café, an army-built replica of an Old West saloon, served by German prisoners of war, whom everyone kept frantically busy with unnecessary orders. When his children were growing up, what partying there was, was done for them; he and his wife celebrated their own birthdays with modest presents and a dinner out. One summer he and his family would have forgotten his birthday except for a telegram from a new friend, who made a point of remembering birthdays. He had his first novel published on his fortieth birthday for two reasons: Oliver Wendell Holmes had said that if you haven't carved your name in the door by forty close up your penknife, and *Ulysses* had been published on Joyce's fortieth birthday. As a secret present to himself he invited his current mistress and her husband to the party. The young woman he fell in love with threw a strenuous party for his fiftieth birthday. All his oldest friends were there; a few had become mild drunks and eccentrics, and everyone except his children reminisced, which left the young woman feeling like a servant: she took it out on him later. His sixtieth birthday neither of his children will attend, the younger being three thousand miles away, the other pleading business in Philadelphia. As time goes on he will realize that his birthdays rather than accomplishments are looked on as postponements.

HE NEVER IMAGINED he was the child of other parents
or what it would be like to be the child of other parents. He never thought his parents didn't want him,
even when they complained about him. When he failed
at something he thought it was his fault, not his parents'. He thought that his parents wished him well: in
fact, that his mother would give up her life for him
and that his father perhaps would not go so far but almost. He never considered what it would be like to
have children himself. When he married he used condoms to relieve his wife of the responsibility of birth
control, which she thought sinful. After a year they
occasionally took a chance without a condom. One such
time he said to his wife, "I think we did it"; and a
few weeks later her pregnancy was confirmed. He

broke the news to his parents by singing at their dinner table, "M is for the million things you gave me . . ." In the first years of their marriage they lived on an island set aside after the war for veterans going to school; it was served hourly by ferry; sometimes, lying abed while his wife and daughter were on the mainland, he pictured his wife running for the ferry, child in arms, jumping to get aboard, and falling into the propeller. He worked for an encyclopedia at the time, and when the project reached Z he was let go. His parents visited him and his wife; his father offered to contribute a weekly sum until he found another job but said that it should be understood this was only being done because a child was involved. He bounced a ping-pong ball through the interview; afterward his wife said she had never been so embarrassed. He and his wife never got enough sleep after their first child was born. At night when the baby went to sleep they would stay up late to enjoy the freedom, then take turns tending it when it woke. He would change a diaper, warm a bottle, for thirty minutes jostle the crib and hum; if the child hadn't gone back to sleep he would return to bed and his wife would take over. The arrival of a second child made things easier: either the children amused one another or he and his wife had exhausted their anxiety over child rearing. One winter morning when he was walking his younger child, a girl, six, plump, and goggle-eyed, to school, he wept: that this child did not have an abler father and that he had not had an abler father. He slipped on the ice and hoped that that would explain the tears if the child noticed them. When his wife asked him to leave home he told his children that he and their mother would no longer be husband and wife but that he would always be their father. The children watched him carefully; he wept throughout the talk. Before he moved out the younger child drew for him a picture of herself sad. He gave it to his mother, whose eyesight was failing; she said it was very nice and hung it in her bedroom. While his children were growing up he stayed in cheap apartments, which one girl friend described as student-sties. When the older child was out of school and the young one near it he allowed himself to fall in love, with a woman much younger than he. Occasionally, feeling great tenderness for her, he would tell her he wanted to have a child with her, and he would picture another daughter like his own but with the advantage of a more experienced father and parents closer together. Now that things do not go well with him and the younger woman, he pictures a son whom the mother would enlist in disputes with him and who would tell him he is useless and should die; sometimes he sees himself dying while the son is young, the son growing up homosexual, becoming famous, and biographies pointing out that the boy was raised by the mother. When he notices the exhaustion of new parents he will congratulate himself that at least in this respect he did the right thing in life by not starting a second family. When his daughters, who will have had many attachments, marry late and the likelihood of their bearing children is past he will have a sense of relief. He will wonder whether they ascribe their childlessness to their early family experiences, also whether they will ever understand how much more important parents are to children than children to parents.

His mother and father told him that children love their parents. His grammar school teachers told him the same thing, adding that the love of children for their parents is like the love of human beings for God. He did not love God or his parents and because of it felt something was wrong with him. The first love he thought of as love was for certain girls. Some of these did not know he loved them. In the sixth grade he sent an unsigned declaration of love to a girl whose father was a prize fighter. She was quiet and gentle, and he considered these qualities all the finer in light of her father's occupation. In the seventh grade he fell in love with a girl named Helen, whom he kissed at graduation parties, took skating, and in the summer named a rowboat after. In the fall, however, she dropped him.

He recognized love by the aura of pleasure that surrounded everything to do with the particular girl: her neighborhood, clothes, friends, books, pets; odd parts of the girl, like the nose and fingernails, seemed perfect. In high school he was always in love with one girl or another, and when he was fourteen he fell in love with the girl he married eight years later. This girl at first was passive and undemonstrative. He thought of her as a clean slate on which he would write his beliefs. She was so much in his mind that when traveling alone around the city he sometimes paid two fares by mistake. When his first child, a girl, was born he was not prepared for the responsibilities of fatherhood, and although she closely resembled him he resented her. But when she began to talk and he saw that her character, too, was like his he began to love her. His second child, also a girl, did not resemble him in any way, and he ignored her. There were so many difficulties in his marriage that after a few years he could not say to himself that he loved his wife. He had an affair with a woman who was also unhappily married. He did not know whether he loved her or not, although many times he told her he did, especially when they were making love. He enjoyed hearing her say that she loved him, but he did not feel the same concern for her that he remembered having felt for his wife. Still, when the affair ended he was bereft and thought that probably he had loved her. After he and his wife were divorced his younger daughter phoned to ask if he loved her. They talked for an hour, wept, and he told her that he did; only then did he know that he did. After his father died he had a recurrent dream in which he tried to save his father from death; sometimes he succeeded, and sometimes he failed; but the dreams were so intense that he came to believe that probably he had loved his father too. As a new bachelor he had many affairs. The sudden release of emotion that accompanied them was gratifying; he wanted to remain capable of it but also keep it under control. He explained to a woman who wished him to love her: "If I love you you will have power over me. If I love you a little you will have a little power over me. If I love you a lot you can kill me." "But why would I kill you if you loved me and I loved you?" He didn't know the answer. "You could love me secretly," she said. "Maybe I do," he said; but he didn't; and, soon after, the affair ended. As he moved from woman to woman he saw that his first feelings about a new woman derived from his last feelings about the previous one, and this knowledge destroyed the effect. One day he had a professional lunch with a young married woman. As he was shown to her table he began to fall in love with her. They talked well, and his love increased in surges, like blood filling an excited penis. During the next two weeks he called her many times a day. He met her after work and drove her home. In the evenings he wrote her long letters and had them delivered by messenger next morning. In his apartment he drank and walked about, raising his hands to the ceiling and making sounds of pain. She left her husband, and they lived together. She is unhappy and yearns for her former life. She criticizes everything he does and everything she considers him to be. She will fall in love with a young widower and leave him. His strongest feelings thereafter will be toward his daughters and toward young men who remind him of his past self.

By turns he was sad and angry that his brother didn't like him and wouldn't play with him. His brother made up sideshow chants about him: "Come see the dog-faced boy! He barks, he bites, he swallows flies." One Christmas he resolved never to speak to his brother again and didn't until the following Christmas, when at the urging of his parents he and his brother exchanged presents. Occasionally his brother defended him against a boy older than he but younger than his brother, and he was filled with pride and gratitude; but ordinarily his brother ignored him. He loved the comic pictures of elephants his brother drew and sometimes gave a week's allowance for one. He coveted all his brother's possessions and couldn't resist bargaining for them. His brother always exacted a high price. Once his brother bought a new outfielder's glove and sold him the old one for three dollars. The first time he took it out a boy offered him five dollars for it; he wanted to keep the glove but took the money so he could brag to his brother about the sharp deal he had made. By the time he and his wife knew one another well he couldn't win a point from her. If she was losing an argument she would become silent and let him talk on without her resistance or agreement. Sometimes she would withdraw from him for no reason. "What did I do?" he would say. "If you don't know I can't help you," she would answer. Often with his wife he felt the same angry breathlessness he had felt as a child talking with his brother and father. After writing a few short stories he realized he wanted to write in order to make one-time statements; if people disagreed with him they could address themselves to the statements: he would not have to repeat himself. Later he wondered if this motive limited his output. After years of trying to please his boss, the boss, as retirement approached, backed another man to take over. His anger woke him at night; he talked compulsively against the boss to strangers and later learned that at social gatherings people had put him on by mentioning the boss's name and then stepping back to see him perform. The young woman he fell in love with had fits of anger. While still married she visited him one Christmas week to make cookies with him and suddenly shouted, "Don't watch *me,* do it *yourself!*" He called her Cookie Monster for a few days thereafter, which helped him get over the incident. One morning when they were living together he pointed to her nipples, which showed through her dress with unusual prominence; she struck him on the face, and he felt like a naughty child. She is impelled to denigrate him in front of her friends, telling him that he is drunk and should go to bed, reciting demeaning anecdotes about him, correcting details in his stories. He tries being quiet, also expansive and entertaining; but at some time in the evening she always attacks him, after which she seems released. He no longer gets angry on these occasions, instead watches the reactions of guests, sometimes exchanging a quick smile with one of them. His mother shouts at her ceiling, "Shut up, up there!", then explains that a child in the apartment above follows her from room to room to torment her. When he places phone calls for her, if the party doesn't answer and he dials again she shouts, "That's *enough.* We'll stop that right *now.*" He remembers her as a placid person and wonders what these outbursts mean: are they repressed anger from her past; and if he lives long enough will contained feelings come from him like this? When his mother dies he will be less upset than his brother, who will lose his temper with him and the funeral director over details of the funeral. He will recall how upset he was at his father's death, publicly pulling away from his wife when she tried to take his arm in a comforting gesture. He will realize that it is easier to lose the parent that favored one than the parent that didn't.

HE WANTED TO DO what older people did, but he did not want to be like them. He did not want to be like his father, who had no fun; or his brother, who kept to himself and grunted when thinking; or his parents' male friends, who rose from chairs with difficulty; or priests, who had bad manners and stains on their clothing. His mother had pretty skin, enjoyed jokes, and was pleasant to his friends; some other mothers were even nicer than his mother: but mothers were women. What he wanted was to stay up late, go out alone, make money, and buy things. He knew that by getting older he would be able to do this; still, he didn't want to go to kindergarten, because his mother would have to leave him there. The first day, the kindergarten class visited the park and sang "Frère Jacques," which he liked.

"After the summer," his mother said, "when you go to the real school I'll buy you a sailor suit." She did, and also a pencil case containing three yellow pencils, a pencil sharpener, a protractor, a six-inch wooden ruler, and an eraser, one end of which was soft for pencil and the other hard for ink. He looked forward to the fifth grade, where he would wear a uniform of gray tunic with stiff collar, gray pants, and a hard gray cap with a shiny black peak. If he went to his brother's high school he would learn Latin and Greek. "Latin is hard," his brother said, "but nothing like Greek," and his brother drew the Greek characters that meant "the sea, the sea." Among his brother's college books was *The Theory of the Leisure Class* in a small green edition with a figure of a naked woman carrying a torch stamped in gold on the spine. He kept it in his room; his brother didn't miss it. Six months before starting college he had read the catalogue thoroughly and wanted to elect twice as many courses as allowed. By his second term he yearned to be in the army: there would be no homework, he would live outdoors, and he would get laid. After three days the army seemed dangerous and demeaning, and he held himself apart so it would not change him. For the first time in his life he wanted to be younger than he was, and he day-dreamed of being wakened in the morning by his mother holding a glass of orange juice. At night his nonsexual dreams were of real, past, personal events. He told himself that if in the future he should ever be about to think that the army was not so bad he must remember what he thought now: that it is the worst time of his life (and he has not forgotten this). When he was discharged he wanted to finish college, get a job, and marry. When his marriage began to fail he thought that to be free of the hostile presence of his wife and able to take out other women openly and guiltlessly would make him happy. When he left home he lived in a small apartment in a poor neighborhood, pressed his clothes after cleaning them with spot remover, and cooked meals of cheap food. After his children were almost grown he fell in love with a young woman. Their initial passionate lovemaking is degenerating into importunity and accommodation. Although the relationship has lessened his self-regard, his potency, and the affection of his friends (whom she snubs) he dreads losing her. After they separate he will no longer wish to move into the future; he will try to pamper himself by searching among unsatisfied desires of his childhood and adolescence for things to spend money on: he will buy a powerful microscope, planning to see for the first time what magnified blood and sperm look like, but will lose the impulse because it will not seem to matter what they look like; and white bucks with red rubber soles, which will amuse his friends but which he will be embarrassed to wear among strangers. He will buy the complete works of Freud, thinking that he might read them one at a time, to the exclusion of other books, and write a response in the manner of Norman O. Brown. As his functions fail he will blame recent minor illnesses rather than age and claim that soon again he will be able to go out by himself, prepare bachelor meals for his friends, take care of his finances; when he explains this to his daughters they will become silent and he will have a restless night.

IF HE WAS TOLD not to cross a certain street or play with certain friends and wanted to, he would anyway. If he was asked then whether he had, he would lie. When he was old enough to shop by himself he sometimes took coins from his mother's purse or from the change his father spread on the bureau after getting home from work. He wrote spelling lists in a fine hand on small pieces of paper, intending to consult them during tests; usually the act of writing was enough to make him remember the spelling. When he began to study geography he bought a pocket loose-leaf notebook and traced in it maps of countries, one to a page, noting on the maps the major cities and beneath the maps the national products. He kept the book between his legs during tests and was so adept at using it not even the other students knew about it. In his last year of grammar school he played cards for money on the sidewalk. The favorite game was banker and broker. Every few days he would put a new deck into play. After an hour it would be scuffed from the concrete. In the evening he would further scrape the corners of the face cards and aces. He would put the deck back into play the next day, and from the corners of the bottom cards he could pick the winning piles. One day when he was banker and the pot was high a black boy asked him if he could run fast. He said no; the boy scooped up the money and ran. The other players were surprised that he was amused. After a few weeks he gave the game up out of anxiety and boredom. In high school he could learn Latin but not Greek. For final tests in Greek he cut the pages from a translation of the term's text—Xenophon's *Anabasis*, say—putting Book One in the right-hand side pocket of his jacket, Book Two in the left, Book Three in the inside pocket, and so on; and when the lines to be translated were announced by the proctor he would take out the appropriate pages and slip them under the test paper. In this way he did as well in Greek as in Latin. On one test he caught a proctor observing him cheat; the proctor didn't turn him in, and later he wondered whether the reason had been sympathy or apathy. When he began having adulterous affairs he often lied to his wife about where he had been or where he was going; otherwise he told her the truth, even concerning his opinions about her. Once in anger she said to him that there was nothing he wouldn't say. He knew that it would often be convenient to lie, but he thought people would be able to detect it. When he was seeing an analyst he developed the theory that the habit of repression is due to children feeling that parents can read their minds. One day a book critic, confident of an affirmative answer, asked him if he didn't think true novelists enjoyed lying. He said no, he told the truth whenever he could. The critic did not press the point, but he could see that the critic preferred to maintain the notion rather than think of him as a novelist. When asked, he has told writers what he thinks of their work, unless it is very bad, in which case he has praised it. On another day, at lunch, a novelist asked him if he thought his books were better than the novelist's. He said indeed he did. Then, wanting to soften the judgment, he added that their books were not comparable: "Mine are literary, yours are not," he said. "What do you mean by *that?*" the novelist said. "Mine are written in a certain style; all the styles they are not written in are implied by not being used. Your books are catch-as-catch-can." "Well, fuck you!" the novelist said and left the table. A woman friend he told this to said, "He wanted to know whether you thought yours was bigger than his. He should just come out of the closet and settle down." He and the novelist did not speak for a year; then one day the novelist asked him out for a drink and said that it had become clear that his remarks about their books had been hostile. "Why would I have been hostile?" he said. "Because you were jealous," the novelist said. "Why would I have been jealous?" "Because I'm better-looking," the novelist said. He avoided the novelist completely thereafter. Once in Rome with an English girl he cashed an American traveler's check in the train station. A few minutes later he was summoned to the exchange by loudspeaker. The clerk said he had taken too many lire. He said he was sorry, he had not done it on purpose, and returned the overpayment. The girl said he was a fool for having given back the money and especially for apologizing. "It would have paid for another day here," she said. He half agreed with her but never felt the same about her afterward. He continues to be honest and forthright and thinks that the world would be better without lies and self-deception. However, later he will meet and mix with well-off people and will be struck by the fact that neither they nor their servants want to see the implication of the relation. More than anything else this will convince him that although honesty is possible to some people and attractive when achieved it is not a natural human quality. One of his friends will die from cancer and will have known from the initial diagnosis that he would die. Near death, although not in pain or anticipation of pain, the friend will say, "As soon as the doctor knew, he should have told me the tests were negative and put me to sleep like a cat."

Doctors had deep voices and hair on the backs of their hands. When he passed an apartment with its door ajar and heard a deep voice he knew it was a doctor, hand on knob, ready to leave, giving final advice. His mother talked a lot about doctors. Her favorite was their pediatrician, who she claimed had saved his brother's life when his brother was an infant by replacing a formula prescribed by another doctor with whole milk, on which his brother thrived. This pediatrician was gruff with him and pleasant to his mother. In the pediatrician's office the nurse would tell him to take off all his clothes except his socks. She would weigh and measure him and put him on the edge of a cold, leather examining table to wait. When the doctor arrived his mother would tell how he had eaten, slept, moved his bowels, breathed, played, and felt since his last visit. The doctor would tap his knee, look up his nose, down his throat, into his ears and eyes, and lift his testicles while he coughed and sweat rolled from his armpits over his ribs. One day when he was seven the doctor told him to remove his right sock, pricked his big toe, and touched a piece of glass to the spot of blood. That evening his father brought him home a new bathrobe. The next morning his mother packed it in a case with a pair of pajamas. They were going to the hospital, she said, so the doctor could look at the toe. He became suspicious when he saw his father waiting for them at the hospital, and he was panicked when he was made to change into his pajamas. It took two male attendants and three nurses to get him onto the operating table. When he woke they gave him vanilla ice cream and told him that his tonsils had been removed. Five years later he had acute appendicitis and was so sick he hardly cared what happened to him. As a nurse was shaving his stomach and the surgeon looked on he asked the surgeon the death rate in appendectomies. One in fifty, the surgeon said; this seemed an acceptable risk, and he proposed a deal: he would not struggle on the table if the surgeon would not restrain him. The surgeon agreed, and they both kept their word, although as he was breathing the anesthetic he changed his mind but found that his arms were numb. One day in his office when he was thirty his heart began to pound; he thought he was having a heart attack and took a taxi home. His family doctor assured him that nothing was wrong; he went to a heart specialist, who said the same thing. He told the heart specialist that he was sure he was going to die and that the heart specialist was lying to save him anguish in his last days. The heart specialist sent him to a psychiatrist, who looked like his brother and in the subsequent five years of treatment said very little. He tried to engage the psychiatrist in arguments on public and private matters, insulted the psychiatrist, occasionally gave the psychiatrist presents, pointed out inconsistencies in the few things the psychiatrist said, but never elicited much response. If he told a joke the psychiatrist smiled; if he laughed the psychiatrist laughed. One day after recounting a sexual fantasy he accused the psychiatrist of blushing. "I'm not blushing," the psychiatrist said, "you are"; and indeed his face was burning. On one visit the psychiatrist took notes, something the psychiatrist had not done since the initial interview years before. Sarcastically he asked if the psychiatrist was drawing his picture. "Why do you think I'm drawing your picture?" the psychiatrist said, and he understood in a new way that psychiatry could be a serious business. The most valuable lesson of the treatment came from the psychiatrist's silence: one did not have to talk; one could listen, and others didn't mind. He still regularly sees the heart specialist, who takes his blood pressure, listens to his chest, and chats with him for half an hour. The heart specialist will age, wander in his talk, and never find anything wrong with him. Guiltily he will visit another doctor, younger than himself, explain that he wants to continue seeing the heart specialist but also wants scientific care. The new doctor will say, "But you are going to him for his sake, not yours." He will nod. "Well, if that's what you want." This will be the first of a series of doctors younger than himself, and when the heart specialist retires he will realize that the appeal of having a doctor older than oneself is the appeal of having an expert between oneself and death.

His closest summer friend was Robert, who was thoughtful and plump and had a twin sister, who was thin and boyish and the only girl who could beat him up. Like most of his friends Robert was older than he. Robert helped him learn to swim, taught him tennis and chess, and resisted others who wanted to exclude him from games because of his age. Robert did things he thought admirable but odd, like keeping a twice-daily record of home barometer readings and using only one piece of toilet paper after defecating. Robert had a strong sense of right and wrong and was accepted as a leader because of it. One day when he and Robert were taking turns shooting Robert's BB gun on the beach Robert killed a sea gull. Robert made him promise not to tell anyone (and for a long time he didn't). As Robert got better at chess he got better, but he could not beat Robert. Then one day at midgame he saw more future moves than usual and won. Robert challenged him to another game, which he also won. He thought Robert would be pleased, but Robert was angry and silent. He thought he would never lose to Robert again, but the next day Robert beat him three times. His second closest summer friend was James, who was not so good at chess as Robert but whom he could not beat. One day Robert suggested a trick: the next time he played James, Robert would sit behind him as a spectator; he would pass his hand slowly over the board, and when it was nearest to the piece to move Robert would tap him on the back. He would then test the piece in the available squares, and at the right one Robert would tap him again. In this way he beat James game after game for a week. James gave chess up and would not even watch when he and Robert played thereafter. Robert felt bad about the trick and tried to lure James back but couldn't. When he was twelve and Robert fifteen they began to discuss religion. Robert believed in God, whereas he himself had doubts. He could not convince Robert of his viewpoint even though Robert could not answer his arguments. They also talked about sex: Robert took the Catholic line that all sex outside marriage and not for procreation was wrong. He more and more doubted this, and they finally dropped the subject. One day on the beach James's sister Sue, a faintly pretty girl, asked him to find out what Robert thought of her. She said she cared for Robert but suspected that Robert did not care for her, because her breath was bad. He said he would talk to Robert but also he would test her breath there and then. She blew into his face; her breath was sweet. He got an erection and, excusing himself, went into the ocean and stayed there until the erection was gone. He asked Robert about Sue, and Robert said he liked her. He reported this to Sue, and that was the last he heard of it. During the summer between Robert's junior and senior high school years Robert kept to himself, took walks alone along the shore, didn't go to the movies or beach parties or on the evening visit to the ice cream parlor. The next summer, after Robert's graduation, Robert announced that in the fall he would be entering the priesthood. Robert was friendlier then, but he and the others were uncomfortable now that they knew Robert was to become a priest. One day when they were sitting in the shade of Robert's bungalow playing word games those opposite Robert saw that one of Robert's testicles was exposed, caught between leg and bathing suit. At a covert conference on the far side of the bungalow Sue was picked to explain the situation to Robert. She whispered into Robert's ear; Robert disappeared into his bungalow and was not seen for two days. When the war started, everyone but Robert went into the service. After the war Robert was sent to the Philippines to teach. He heard from his mother that Robert had not wanted to go abroad. He also heard that Robert had become principal of a Philippine school; he was not surprised, because Robert had always struck everyone as a born leader. Eventually Robert was returned to the States. When Robert was thirty-nine, he thirty-six, married, with two children, he had dinner with Robert. It was the first time he had seen Robert since Robert became a priest. He was taken aback at how small and passive Robert was and at the homey quality of Robert's speech; he remembered Robert as sure, severe, and elegant. In his first novel, for reasons he did not understand, he represented Robert as a comic, neuter character. Since then he has avoided meeting Robert. Robert is now the chaplain in a local prison, and through bits of information he understands that Robert has a drinking problem. Robert's twin sister, he will learn, is happy as a Madam of the Sacred Heart and is the author of influential papers on the teaching of mathematics. Sue will die in a public institution after schizophrenic disintegration. He will wonder if she and Robert would have done better had they gotten together and will decide no.

WHEN HE WAS ABOUT TO BE TAKEN to his first movie he asked his mother what movies were like. "They're dark in one place and light in another," she said. The movie, with Jack Oakie, concerned sailors. Soon after, he was taken to see *The Bat Whispers,* in which a man in a cloak turned into a bat. That night he dreamed he was lying awake in his bed in his room, and into the doorway came an upright figure in a black cloak and slouch hat, with a wolf's face. He spent the rest of the night in his parents' bed. His mother took him to the movies every Friday evening; they went to the same theater, no matter what was playing. On the way home they bought a box of wheat biscuits he especially liked and always arrived in time to hear "The Witch's Tale," the scariest program on radio. While he listened his mother had to stay in sight and he ate a wheat biscuit covered with butter. On Saturday afternoons when he was older he went to a poor, nearby neighborhood where there was a theater named the Hub, which showed three features, serials, cartoons, and newsreels, and charged ten cents. The program started at noon and let out between five and six. He and his friends brought their cap pistols to shoot during the Westerns, cut leather from the seats to use in slingshots, and pissed on the floor of the men's room. On the way home they roamed the streets and went into stores, the braver boys shoplifting in the five-and-ten. One spring dusk they plucked rolls of toilet paper from a display in front of a grocery, undid them, and let them unroll side by side down a hill past the store to see whose would reach the bottom first. In his summer community there was one movie house, with a tin roof, and on rainy days no one could hear the sound track. The bill changed Mondays, Wednesdays, and Fridays; and not a week went by that he did not feel he had to see at least two of the shows, particularly anything with Edmund Lowe, Jack Holt, or Laurel and Hardy. His mother tried to restrict him to one show a week, but by wheedling or deceit he had his way. During his last year in grammar school a local theater named the Casino got a reputation as a place to neck in on Saturday afternoons; he and his friends tried it occasionally, realizing finally that you had to bring your own girl. Word of the Casino reached the pastor of the local Catholic church, who complained to the manager, who hired a matron to walk the aisles of the balcony with a flashlight. In high school he and his first serious girl friend discovered foreign films; even those they didn't enjoy were superior to American films, they maintained. He went one day with his friend Alec to see *Daybreak*, with Jean Gabin; midway the actress Arletty stepped from the shower for an instant of frontal nudity. It was so quick and they were so surprised neither knew he had not imagined it until they checked with one another; they stayed to see the picture again, but the frame or frames were missing the second time. In movie houses on army posts WACs and male officers sat together in sections barred to enlisted men. One evening while he was waiting for the lights to go out and the movie to start an enlisted man inflated a condom and sent it up like a balloon; other soldiers did the same, and soon the house was filled with bobbing condoms. One by one the WACs and male officers left, the enlisted men cheering as they went. One night after seeing a Mickey Spillane movie he and his wife were waiting for the train on a subway platform. What he took for a single car collecting the day's receipts pulled slowly into the station. Suddenly he was sure there would be a robbery: he remembered having noticed men carefully spaced waiting on the stairs near the change booth and along the platform. Instead of stopping, the train speeded up. He thought he heard shots, pushed his wife against the wall, and covered her with his body. When he pulled away he saw that no one was disturbed, and if they had noticed probably thought he and his wife were necking. At a drunken party he was introduced to a well-known woman film critic. He said he wanted to test her taste and put to her pairs for preference. He agreed with all her choices and finally said, "Ritz Brothers, Marx Brothers." "Ritz," she shouted; they embraced and pledged friendship for life. She invited him soon after to see *Deep Throat,* giggled throughout, and was shushed by men in the audience. As they were leaving the theater they walked through a narrow passage by the men's room; a burly, pimpled boy emerged and rubbed himself against her. She elbowed the boy in the chest and giggled. This was the first pornographic film he had seen, and later at dinner she said he was lucky to have lost his cherry with one of the best. Now only at the invitation of others does he go to a movie. Occasionally he watches movies on television; sometimes, if he is drinking, one after the other till dawn. The older he gets the more difficult it will become to be drawn into a movie's fiction: either he has seen similar movies before or the movie maker seems to know less about life than he.

In summer the boys and fathers worked with wood. The fathers made benches, porches, awnings, walks, steps, railings. He made toy boats. From a piece of pine one inch thick and four inches wide he would cut a ten-inch length, sawing one end to a point and tapering the other with a plane. For a second deck he would nail on a smaller piece of the same wood and make smokestacks from sections of broomstick cut at an angle to tilt backwards. If the boat was too high it capsized. Sometimes his brother made a boat for him, and sometimes he made a boat for a younger boy. Behind the general store were discarded wooden crates with one-by-two-inch frames; he and the other boys made guns from the frames by cutting off right-angle pieces with four-inch handles and eight-inch barrels. A rubber band, attached by a staple to the underside of the barrel, was drawn over the end and top of the barrel and fixed at the joint. An inch square of cardboard was inserted on top of the barrel, between the strands of the rubber band, which when released by thumb projected the cardboard fifteen or twenty feet. For a time linoleum squares were used, but abandoned when one, shot at close range, stuck in a boy's back. His brother and father made shoe boxes, toolboxes, shelves; and replaced splintered, broken, and rotten wood in the bungalow. Among their tools were saws, planes, hammers, a hatchet, manual drills, and a Yankee screwdriver, which were oiled, cleaned, or sharpened, carefully stored, and frequently discussed. As the youngest he was allowed to scrape peeling paint from walls and ceilings and under his father's or brother's supervision apply new paint. In the city he made model airplanes from kits that provided plans, balsa wood parts, and glue that smelled like ether. His planes were never so successful as his brother's: the struts dried crooked and lumps of hardened glue disfigured the joints. Into his first novel he put a comic character, based on his brother, who made boxes for inappropriate objects and then boxes for the boxes. One evening while he was working on the novel his brother had an emergency operation; immediately he excised the passages about the character in case his brother and he should die and the unfinished novel be published posthumously. He liked to take his daughters walking in parks and from fallen or new-cut branches make them walking sticks on which he carved designs by stripping the bark in spirals and crosses. He told his daughters the designs were secret American Indian motifs; he didn't know his daughters believed him until a friend of his older daughter asked him one day which tribes the designs came from. His daughters collected the sticks until they became so numerous his wife threw them out. After he left his family he took over the studio of an artist friend, who showed him how to make bookcases, tables, and simple cabinets. He had trouble writing at the time and kept busy by buying slabs of oak and sanding them for table tops. He made more tables than he had room for and gave the excess like kittens to friends. When a table came out well he sometimes sat up drinking, waiting for the varnish to dry, and wished his father were alive to see it. He tried to elicit praise for his work from his brother, but his brother disapproved of his having left his family and of everything that had come of it; also by then his brother had a cellar workshop, was making replicas of antique furniture, and was not impressed. When he fell in love and took an apartment with the woman he made things of wood for her. She asked for a high triangular table to fit between and serve the re-frigerator and stove. He made it with an inch-thick plywood top and four-by-four legs, and it wobbled. Later in a drunken rage he will destroy it. Although he will stop working with wood he will like the feel and look of well-made doors, casements, floors, desks, and chairs and will be contemptuous of veneers and deceptively finished softwoods. He will develop a strong preference for things made of organic materials and be convinced—when he is drunk he will talk about it—that doormats, telephone poles, newspapers, tires, and such are blessed to have escaped being made of plastic. A friend will say, "How about people? They're as organic as you get." "They move," he will say.

If his father left a cigarette butt in the toilet bowl he tried to break it up with a stream of urine. He and his friends urinated in arcs to see whose would go higher. Projective devices like bows and arrows, peashooters, and slingshots were banned in his neighborhood, but a boy from another neighborhood would visit with a BB gun and let him use it. Its kick and the sure sound of the BB hitting a bottle, can, or tree, or merely the idea of the BB flying off in the air filled him with satisfaction. His older brother acquired a .22-caliber rifle to shoot in deserted areas around their summer place; he was forbidden to touch it. When no one was home he would play with it, although his brother had removed and hidden the firing pin. He liked to fling clamshells into the wind so that they bucked and stayed aloft, or with the wind, which lengthened their flight two- or three-fold. He scaled flat stones on calm water, watching them hop till spent. In winter he dropped snowballs from his window, sometimes on passers-by. As the weather warmed he stored snowballs in the freezer for later use. Once, after a heavy snow and partial thaw, the temperature dropped again and the surface snow froze into an icy crust. He and his friends went to the roof of their apartment house, broke off foot-square chunks, and heaved them over the edge. One of them hit a convertible and broke through the canvas top. Screaming with fright and joy, they ran down to the street, but the car was gone. From his uncle, who died suddenly, he inherited fine pinch-nosed pliers, with which he cut copper wire into half-inch pieces and bent them into U-shaped pellets, which he shot with a rubber band at objects and people. When there was no snow he dropped marbles from his window; if they didn't break they bounced high off the sidewalk. When he masturbated, the initial spurt of semen would sometimes form two connected globules, which would swing around one another like twin stars, followed by two or three spurts of diminishing thrust and mass. A rage for water guns took over his freshman high school class, so that students put milk containers filled with water into their desks and through unused inkwell holes drew water to squirt at one another. One day while a teacher was writing on the blackboard he squirted water on the gray slate, which turned black in inverted peaks as the water ran downward. On the Fourth of July the summer he was fourteen he took six skyrockets apart, noting how they were made, and constructed one big rocket with tape and cardboard; it went off in a bright blaze on the ground. Before he reached the age at which his brother had been allowed a rifle he went into the army. The weight, appearance, noise, smell, purpose, and care of the army rifle made shooting it unpleasant for him. After the armistice he and another soldier urinated into the barrels of their rifles the night before the rifles were to be turned in for the last time. He plays tennis now, and once in a while almost every shot of a game seems perfectly hit, the ball springing low and hard from the center of the racket. He will consider keeping a rifle in his apartment against intruders, but the thought that he might become depressed and commit suicide with it will dissuade him. He will throw back to children balls that roll to his feet in the park and ask himself if the children note an eagerness he remembers in the faces of old men returning balls to him when he was a child. Occasionally in the morning he will wonder if he could urinate out the chest-high window above the toilet bowl in his bathroom; he will not try it although he will at times slowly retreat from the bowl to see what thrust is left to him.

In the beginning he was pushed and pulled in a wicker baby carriage. He first moved himself mechanically by pedaling a borrowed toy auto. His first tricycle had a horn with a black squeeze bulb; his second a thumb-operated bell, which he preferred because he didn't have to let go of the handlebars to sound it. All told, he had four tricycles, getting a new one each time he became too tall to pedal comfortably. He used his last tricycle mostly for coasting, riding down the long hill beside his apartment house, legs held out to avoid the spinning pedals. He taught himself to roller-skate by walking on the skates with a heavy step so the wheels wouldn't turn, then by pulling himself along rails and walls. When his brother built a large surfboard of canvas-covered balsa wood he was given his brother's small solid-pine board, on which he rode modest waves near shore. He liked being in his brother's sailboat; the thought, when the boat was becalmed, that eventually there would be wind and then more wind reassured him about the future. In fall and spring he went on slides and swings in playgrounds. It was said that by methodical increase of momentum one could turn full circle in a swing, but he never saw anyone do it, and his own attempts failed when, after he reached heights of forty-five degrees or so above the bar, centrifugal force slackened and the swing dropped with a lurching snap. In early winter he and his friends fitted discarded license plates onto roller skates, sat on the plates, feet tucked up, and rode down steep empty streets, steering by leaning to one side, and ditching one another like stock car racers. He liked to ice-skate and was good at it. He fell on the ice one day, cutting the inside of his left wrist with a skate blade. He later showed the scar to a girl as evidence of a suicide attempt. The first time he went horseback riding he asked for the mildest horse in the stable and was given a nag with a sunken middle and a sly look. As soon as he and his companions were on the trail the horse turned back. He pulled one rein, then the other; finally he held a rein so tight that the horse's head was forced about; still the horse continued to the stable. He declined the offer of another mount and waited for his friends. In the army he joined the paratroopers, made one practice jump, decided that air was an unnatural medium for human locomotion, and quit. He taught himself to drive by practicing on an army Jeep in a parking area for hours. He and another soldier, also learning to drive, took the Jeep out one night and ran it into the officers' barracks at thirty miles an hour. After being taken to the hospital and examined they were put into the stockade and held for misappropriation of government property; but the war was almost over, and no one seemed interested in pressing charges. He bought his first car for one hundred dollars, a 1939 black Ford salesman's coupe, so called because it had one seat and a large trunk. He had been put off by army authority and used the car for two years without license or registration. One night at a party to which he had gone without his wife he dropped an ice cube down the front of the dress of a married woman he knew slightly. She was there without her husband, was amused, which surprised him, and suggested they go to her apartment. On the way there his car struck another car stopped at a red light; she was thrown against the dashboard, he cut his nose on the rearview mirror. They tried to make love at her apartment, but she complained of pain and he was impotent, for the first time in his life. The next day she called to say that three of her ribs were broken and asked him not to tell anyone about the evening. When his first novel was published the woman's husband reviewed it with inappropriate harshness. After countless traffic tickets for moving and standing violations, some of which he paid immediately and some late, he one day decided to obey the law meticulously and hasn't had a ticket since. He will take riding lessons, hoping to please a woman he has fallen in love with, an expert rider. His teacher, either misjudging his experience, sensing his eagerness, or wanting to embarrass him, will make him canter and gallop on the first lesson. Though frightened, he will be exhilarated and successful. He will admire the mass and power of horses but despise their peevishness and servility. When the young woman refuses to ride with him or explain why she won't he will give the sport up. His need for exercise and taste for movement will diminish to the point that he will not leave his home on weekends if he can help it.

HE WAS AFRAID OF BUGS and could bear to touch only those considered playthings, like ladybugs, June bugs, houseflies. Spiders, roaches, mosquito hawks, and beetles made him panicky indoors and uneasy outdoors. Fish and rodents meant little to him because they lacked individuality. Birds were good to watch in flight and admire for their form and color in cages, but they, too, lacked individuality. As a child the only pets he was allowed were impersonal—goldfish, turtles, salamanders. During his ninth summer he put out a dish of milk for a black cat with a white spot on its neck. "You'll never get rid of it," his mother said. It was his intention to keep the cat, and at summer's end he pleaded with his mother to take it back to the city. He had heard that abandoned summer cats died in the winter and used this as an argument, but the argument failed. When he was eighteen he went on a camping trip with two friends. It rained the whole time, and the three of them stayed in their tent. The inside top of the tent was covered with insects. Often in the day he lay on his bunk and watched them crawl over and around one another, fly off the canvas and back again; he felt at home with these insects because the woods were their natural place. When he went into the army he saw many bugs. One day as he crouched in a training foxhole, only his head above ground, a large spider with hairy legs walked within a few inches of his face. He contemplated the spider, and the spider appeared to contemplate him. He was so unhappy in the army that all extramilitary organisms, even plants, seemed more fortunate than he, and he respected them on that account. He had been thinking of masturbating and decided to fuck the spider, after a fashion. He stood up, took out his penis, and rested it on the edge of the foxhole. After slow, methodical manipulation he ejaculated and hit the spider with two of the three expulsions of semen. The spider collapsed into a ball, then righted itself and hurried away. Shortly after his marriage he and his wife spent a weekend at a hunters' cottage. On the second day he saw his wife walking toward him over a small bridge. Her carriage was unusually straight. She hissed his name in fright. "Get it away!"

she said, breaking for the cottage. Behind her loped a large German shepherd. He clicked his tongue, and the dog veered from his wife's trail and came to him. He felt that the dog's interest in his wife was the same as his. He held his arm out like a stick, and the dog took it between its teeth. He crouched down and put out his palms for the dog's paws. The dog offered one paw, but instead of taking it he grabbed the dog's ankles and threw it on its flank. The dog sprang up in a squirming, bounding motion and rose over him on its hind legs. He took the dog around its middle. They wrestled in this way, the dog showing by its growls when he was going too far. During their grappling and turning he noticed his wife watching from a cottage window. He thought she must consider him very brave. Later she made no comment and only nodded when he mentioned the dog. Years later he took to wrestling with a large boxer that belonged to friends. The dog weighed ninety pounds and seemed all muscle and bone. After fifteen minutes or so, always when he was on the point of exhaustion, the dog let itself be pinned like a calf for branding. One evening at the house of these friends a vet told him that an excited dog of this size could have a sudden change of mood and take off an arm in a bite. He was sure he had understood the dog but nevertheless did not wrestle with it again. The dog eventually became blind and feeble, its eyes milky brown; it bumped into furniture, barked at phantoms, and failed to recognize him. He suggested to his friends that they get it a Seeing Eye man; they were shocked at the remark, and he was ashamed. When the dog died it was replaced by a frantic Weimaraner, which he would have nothing to do with. For company after he left his family his daughters got him a cat from a pound; they named it Filia and were very interested in his attitude toward it. One evening it tried to jump into his lap and fell back. He picked it up, it seemed unusually light; he took it to the ASPCA, where he was told it had a wasting disease and should be put to sleep. His daughters got him another cat, which they named Amicus; it lived till they were grown. When he fell in love with a young woman and she moved in with him she brought her cat. She addressed it only by newly invented names—Mousepaws, Tigerlips, Furflinger. As the relationship disintegrates her tone to him will become strident and remain caressing to the cat. Occasionally he will yearn for affection and mistake, for an instant, a word to the cat for a word to him. One Saturday when he is living alone he will see a golden bird hovering, he will think, outside his living-room window; as he approaches he will realize he has misjudged the distance, and the bird is inside. He will open the *I Ching* at random and interpret the verse as saying that the relationship should end and there will be no blame. He will open the book to another page; the verse will seem even clearer: the visitor should go south. With the help of a towel he will force the bird from the window, be relieved that he will not have to take care of it, and understand that the function of the *I Ching* is to enable one to do what one would not ordinarily do.

THE FIRST TIME he wore his Boy Scout uniform a nattily dressed Negro man stopped him on the street and asked him if he wanted to make a dollar. "Doing what?" he said. "Let me jerk you off." "No, *sir,*" he said and hurried away. When he was ten, Fritzie, an older boy with high color and wet lips, began hanging around the neighborhood. He and his friends tolerated Fritzie because Fritzie talked about philosophy and played the harmonica. Fritzie was said to be epileptic although no one had seen him have a fit. One day when he and Fritzie were lying on the grass in a park Fritzie suggested playing with his genitals through his pants. Fritzie said he would like it. He let Fritzie do it but felt no sensation. Fritzie said this was odd and when a boy and girl sat down near them gave it up. He and his friends often expressed the wish that a particular one of themselves were a girl. "Boy, would I fuck you!" they'd say, and the boy who the others wished was a girl would shrug. When he was eleven he and his closest city friend considered serial, mutual anal intercourse or intercourse by insertion of the penis, lubricated, between the legs beneath the anus, but they decided that what they really wanted was a girl and they would wait. In high school near the end of sophomore year Mr. Kendall, a teacher of Greek who had been crippled by polio and used a cane, chose him for Kendall's Kinder, a small group of students who frequented Mr. Kendall's bachelor quarters, where they smoked, gossiped, drank, and listened to Mr. Kendall's observations on life. New members often had not drunk before or had been developing a taste for drinks like Tom Collinses and port wine; Mr. Kendall said that if he did nothing else for his boys he taught them to drink scotch. In the spring of his junior year Mr. Kendall and Mr. Whelan, a teacher of French, invited four members of the group to a weekend in an isolated cabin owned by Mr. Whelan. On Saturday night everyone got drunk, or seemed to, and at midnight Mr. Kendall began shouting, "Who wants to get fucked?" No one wanted to, as far as he knew. He slept in the front seat of Mr. Kendall's car, another boy slept in the back, and they all returned to the city early next morning. In the army he met the first acknowledged homosexual he liked, a tall boy with bright eyes who wanted to be called by his last name, Pearl. Pearl stooped to be shorter and claimed that his only argument with the army was that it had developed his leg muscles. He was not put off by Pearl, because Pearl seemed to be imitating a homosexual, whereas Pearl's friend Harry, who asked to be called Harriet, seemed to be the real thing. Pearl was full of theories and stories about male homosexuals: the real ones wanted to be women; they desired only men who desired women and thus were destined for frustration; there existed a prize of a million dollars, established anonymously by a homosexual, awaiting the first man to have a baby. Pearl and Harry invited him to visit the house of a civilian homosexual they knew in the town near camp. He accepted and after dinner went to bed with Pearl in a room snugly shuttered and completely dark. He was made to come three times; there had been much shifting around in bed, and afterward he suspected that the host, an ugly man, had changed places with Pearl midway. Next morning Harry brought Pearl a cherry in a glass. The experience had been no more pleasurable to him than masturbation, and he did not sleep with Pearl again. Pearl accepted this, but Harry for weeks afterward pleaded with him to go to bed. The first person he knew with a hyphenated name, a young attractive bachelor, took him up as a confidant and reported regularly on progress in finding a suitable girl friend. He was unhappily married at the time and envied the bachelor's single life until one day the bachelor said, "I haven't had sex in two years, not since I broke up with a dancer friend." "What happened to her?" he asked the bachelor. *"Him,"* the bachelor said, and he realized that sexual confessions contain propositions. The second man he knew with a hyphenated name, who affected intricate designs in facial hair, who was both boyish and avuncular, and who was liked by everyone for a while, prevented a colleague from getting an influential job by telling the employer that the colleague was homosexual. The colleague over drinks at a bar one evening said to him, "He didn't even ask me if I was," and then after a pause, "You know what's the matter with him? He wants to be a good guy but just can't." He is contemptuous of lesbians because they seem angry and not able to do much about it. He thinks male homosexuals are unlucky and damaged. As sex becomes less important to him so will sexual differences: people will seem to be peering through sexual masks they can't remove.

His MOTHER kept an Irish nursemaid when he was a baby. The nursemaid stayed with the family till he was two years old. He remembers her boy friend better than he remembers her. The boy friend was a bus conductor with a red face. The boy friend's job was to stand at the rear of the double-decker bus and collect fares. The nursemaid would wheel the baby carriage to the bus stop at a certain hour and wait for the boy friend. The boy friend had a ticket punch and a change maker. One day the boy friend gave him a violet-flavored Life Saver. This pleased him and made him proud. Shortly afterward the family moved across the river to another apartment house, and the nursemaid left. She went back to Ireland to get married, his mother told him when he was old enough to ask. His mother also said that he began to talk only after the nursemaid had left. His first sentence, his mother said, was, "When are we going to the old home?" What had the nursemaid looked like? he asked his mother. "She was pretty," his mother said. "Did she look like any*body?*" "No," his mother said. He didn't know whether that was good or bad. When he was seven he was given a ticket punch of his own and made quarter-inch holes in many things. One day he looked for the punch, and it was gone. He searched through his possessions but could not find it. Every now and then he yearned for the punch and would go through his things again, certain that a really thorough search would turn it up, but it didn't. Once when he was ten and in a candy store he asked for violet-flavored Life Savers. The candy store man didn't have them and had never heard of them. On the way home he went into a drugstore that had a greater selection of Life Savers and asked the cashier for violet. "You mean grape," the cashier said. "No, violet." "Violet isn't a flavor, it's a color," the cashier said. But he knew exactly how it would taste if he could find it. One evening he visited a show business couple, who after dinner broke out some marijuana. He had never tried it, didn't believe it worked, had been drinking, and smoked both the pipe and the cigarettes that were passed to him. Soon a plant against the wall, as in a movie trick, turned into a church palm. The space in the room divided itself into vertical and horizontal planes. He could focus his attention either deeply and narrowly or broadly and shallowly. Then the room turned into a long tiled path that led back to his birth. High tile walls stood on either side of the path. Above, the sky was clear and blue. The distant tiles, near his birth, were bright yellow and orange. The tiles near him were dirty and dark. The causes of the darkening, many and varied, stood like markers out of sight on the far sides of the walls. He could not see them, but he knew they were there. Suddenly at the far end of the path, the figure of a woman ascended slowly into the sky. He strained to see her face, but either it was averted or it had no features. He understood that her faceless-ness was due to a failure of memory and that the tile-darkening troubles in his life outside the walls were beyond the power of his mind to identify specifically. After the figure had disappeared into the sky a voice said, "It was bad to lose her when you were two, but it has been worse to love her more than your mother." This message struck him as so important and he thought it so likely that he would forget it that he asked the host, who under the influence of marijuana was taking notes like a scientist, to write it on a piece of paper and give the paper to him. Soon he will lunch with a friend, a middle-aged college teacher. He will tell the friend about the experience and show the friend the paper, which he will still be carrying with him in his wallet. The friend will study the paper and say that for the first time he realizes that *he* married his wife because she resembled *his* nursemaid. "Has it been a happy marriage?" he will ask the friend, knowing that it hasn't been; the friend will raise his hand, palm down, tilt it from side to side, and say, "Apparently there are more variations to the Oedipus complex than Freud ever dreamed of in his philosophy." Shortly before his mother dies he will tell her, too, about the experience. He will think that it will be an even more momentous revelation to her than it had been to him. "Oh," his mother will say, "I knew that. She was a very nice girl and *very* fond of you."

THE ORIGINAL BOSS was his father, whom he could not turn from a decision, get praise out of, or beat in an argument. After delivering advice or an admonishment his father would say, "I just want you to be prepared for the world." One day his father recounted an exchange that had occurred at work: "The boss said to me, 'You always say no, you never say yes.' I said to the boss, 'You have plenty of people around here to say yes, how many do you have to say no?' And do you know what the boss said to me? The boss answered, 'How many do I need?'" He nodded, agreeing with the boss's point, which his father did not seem to have understood. When he brought home a good report card his father said, "The marks don't matter so long as you do your best." This was unsatisfying because he was never sure that he had done his best. Still he did not doubt his father's good will. (A psychiatrist later said that his trust of the world was due to his trust of his father—"a considerable gift," the psychiatrist added.) He was expert at getting praise from teachers, being better mannered, spoken, and dressed than most of the students, as well as quicker and pleasanter-looking. And when an occasional teacher did not take to him he did not feel it reflected on him: the teacher either had an odd temperament or was stupid. Not that a teacher's approval gave him much pleasure: if a teacher liked him he usually doubted the teacher's judgment or more likely felt he had misrepresented himself to the teacher. In college he allowed himself to enjoy the approval of one professor of English who liked his themes and then his poetry. Once in conference in the professor's office when he had made a clever remark the professor leaned across the desk and touched the back of his hand. "I was Adam to his God," he told a friend later. The professor died in his senior year, and campus talk made it clear that the professor had been a homosexual. He wondered whether the professor had liked him because the professor was a homosexual or whether it mattered. When he took his first steady job the boss was a large-headed, thick-necked, dainty-fingered, pot-bellied, bad-breathed doctor of philosophy in history who smiled inadvertently at learning of someone's ill luck, had a watery eye, visited distant cities to hear boy choirs, and cleaned his fingernails with a letter opener. One day when he was about to go to lunch with this boss the boss couldn't decide whether to wear a topcoat: "I hate paying a quarter to someone for hanging it up." "Then leave it," he said. "They'll think I'm cheap," the boss said. "They won't notice," he said. "Don't kid yourself," the boss said. The boss ended by not wearing the coat and overtipping the waiter. This boss was incompetent and came in for public criticism, which forced the employer, who did not want to seem weak, to keep the boss in the job till retirement, at which point the boss had a stroke. One day in a restaurant he ran into the boss propped up like a dummy in bright clothes and eating soft food. At the end of a short conversation he said, "It's been good seeing you," and as he walked away the phrase "like this" occurred to him. He made this man a villain in his second novel, which diminished the novel; and he realized that an unresolved, resolvable problem is no subject for fiction. The next boss was a man ten years his junior who preferred to deal with contemporaries. The new boss tried to be the opposite of the predecessor by doing things like listening to and advising on the personal problems of staff members, by soliciting suggestions on professional matters from the nonprofessional help and then apologizing when the suggestions couldn't be used. Having tried to be thought well of by everyone, this boss will quit in exhaustion. The next boss will also be young, and soon a pattern useful to the corporation will be set: young men moving quickly through the job, the job having become a testing place and stepping stone. He will realize that if this had been the case when he was young he would have attached himself to one of the bosses and moved up behind. He will have developed certain skills reputed to be inimitable, so that new bosses, ingratiating themselves with old employees, will say to him things like, "When I was a kid, a *kid,* I knew your work. I may not have known who was doing it, but, by God, I knew *someone* was doing it." One day he will walk into the boss's office and the conversation between the boss and an assistant will stop. The assistant will have been saying, "We can't ask him to do *that,*" and he will realize that they had been talking about him and that he is seen as an aging loser whose illusions about himself should not be disturbed.

His MOTHER told him that people are not what they seem. One fall, returning to the city after the summer, he met a boy a year older than he; the boy had recently moved into the neighborhood, was amusing and good-looking, and liked him. He told his mother that he had made a new best friend, whom he would be friends with always. His mother said that no one yet knew much about the boy's family, and indeed when he first met the boy's parents he was put off that the mother was taller than the father. By the next summer he and the boy hardly spoke to one another. The nuns in grammar school taught that everyone was created by God and endowed with an immortal soul. If some people seemed less attractive and gifted than others, despite God's intention, it occurred to him that the difference might be an illusion. Perhaps the reason adults were so often unpleasant was that they lived their real lives with other adults and were not themselves among children; perhaps ugly, cruel, or stupid children would eventually be changed by intense compensatory love from their parents; perhaps bums had virtues that events would bring out. In grammar school classes there were at least one very good boy and very good girl not smart or lively; teachers and other students used them as examples and even asked their opinions on moral matters. Their goodness showed in their faces; these boys and girls were usually fair and blue-eyed, with a sad and impassive expression. They were often elected to class office, and sex was not discussed in relation to or in front of them. In high school it became hard for him to see what a disagreeable boy's compensating or excusing virtues were. For instance, in senior year when the students voted for the best among themselves in various categories one untalented and hermetic boy voted for himself for best poet. The poems the boy had offered to the school magazine had been ordinary; and the boy had made not one clever remark in or out of class. The other students privy to the vote were amused, but he himself had been elected best poet by an overwhelming majority and thought that for the first time he was seeing a person without redeeming qualities. There was much cruelty in the army; he somewhat excused it by considering that soldiers led an unnatural life. It was difficult to account for the fact that everyone he spoke to, including German POWs, wanted the war to end and yet it did not. Although he had been taught about the devil he had also been taught about individual responsibility, so that he thought it possible that national leaders accounted for evil. In his first serious job he worked under a man who used a fatherly manner on subordinates. This and the subordinates' desire to be in the hands of a just boss led most of them to think well of the man, despite the fact that the man placed people in the wrong jobs so that they would think less of themselves, praised inferior work to disorient superior workers, and resisted suggestions presented with passion. In time the man confessed secret homosexuality, a wife's alcoholism, and that a son (according to a psychiatrist) was full of anger; this was the first person he knew whom he thought evil. He had a literary success, which brought out qualities he had not seen in people before: some fawned on him frightenedly, as if they wanted to avoid being humiliated by him; others waited for signs of overreaching and humiliated him when they occurred; after his marriage broke up he saw that expectations of compensatory justice were being satisfied. One evening, after he had fallen in love and had been shopping with the young woman, they were going to his apartment, their arms full of bundles; they were stopped in the lobby by three black men. He offered his wallet; the leader, holding a gun, refused it and ordered them upstairs into the apartment. He said he wouldn't go. "You want me to blow her brains out?" the leader said. One of the other blacks pricked his neck with a knife and said, "Move!" Still he wouldn't. Two male tenants arrived, and the blacks fled. The next day he decided that if he could kill the black men with impunity he would, shooting them one by one between the eyes. It wasn't that they were evil, but that they were his mortal enemies, having intended degradations worse than death. Less and less will he think of people as good or bad; rather it will seem to him that benefactors look good to the beneficiaries, injurers bad to the injured, and that the rest is taste.

AT HOME he was taught that he could do what he wanted with what was his except destroy it or give it away. At school giving was good: frequent collections were taken for the Foreign Missions, which ministered to poor, usually yellow people; and once a year money was collected for Catholic Charities, a fund for needy local Catholics. The teaching at home closest to charity was not to waste. If you were frying an egg for a sandwich, say, and looking forward to biting the yolk, which would mix with the melting butter and soak into the pores of the bread, and the yolk ruptured in the pan, you ate the broken egg, you did not begin with another. His mother gave his old clothes and those of his brother that could not be handed on to him to the grammar school principal to distribute among families down on their luck. Occasionally he would recognize a piece of his clothing on a boy and wonder if the boy knew where it had come from. He mentioned to his father that to avoid embarrassment the school might exchange its clothing with another school's. His father was impressed with the suggestion and urged him to pass it along to the principal; he felt he had said cleverer things without credit. Panhandlers asked him for money more often when he was with a girl than not, and he gave more often then. The first time he was panhandled by a woman he gave her nothing and later realized he had almost given her all the money with him. When he was first married he and his wife lived in a community of veterans going to college. A couple might suddenly need money—the government check had not come, a baby had to go to the hospital—and a quiet collection was taken up. This was the first charity he thought about and approved of: help to equals. He never knew or heard of anyone aided by organized charities and avoided giving to them if he could. For a while newspapers ran articles about beggars faking incapacities and making big money. He watched beggars bumping and tapping through subway cars, gauged the money collected and the time spent, and concluded their income was probably low. One Christmas Eve when he and his wife were doing last-minute shopping after dinner and snow had begun to fall an unkempt and bearded man walked toward them in the light of store windows. He gave the man a dollar, apologizing as he did. He and his wife watched from the corner: half the passers-by gave the man money, mostly bills. Two years after he left his family, when he was moving from one bachelor apartment to another, to save money he hired hippie movers. He liked them for their beards and easy manner; the next day he discovered they had stolen a carton of his shoes and clothes. That afternoon a drunk on the street asked him for money. "Fuck off!" he said. "God bless you!" the drunk said. One of the neighborhoods he lived in a friend described as for people on the way up or on the way down: he wondered how the friend saw him: early middle-aged, living alone, most of his income going to his former wife for child support. Hung over at work some mornings, he thought it would be easy to be fired, dropped by friends, avoided by relatives, finally supported by his mother and brother with small corrective donations. Because of his Catholic training he had believed that the helpless were blessed; now they seemed self-willed victims. When a beggar asks him for money he walks on, stony-faced, feeling that if he gives even a small amount of his little money he will be drawn down toward the beggar's debasement. When his children are grown and his money free he will see more sense in charity. When he comes across a confused old woman in the streets he will wonder whether she has children somewhere; if so how she came to be separated from them: had she abandoned them young, they her old? He will think how unwanted a woman is who has passed the age of sexual attractiveness and how little camaraderie there is among women, so eager to help children and animals, so slow to help one another: an old woman does not approach a young one the way an alcoholic does a businessman. He will not see himself in the place of old bums; if nothing else they have hair, he'll be bald.

His MOTHER gave him everything he wanted, within reason, so that he became careful not to take advantage of her. Some days he would stay home after school and follow after the woman who helped his mother clean and cook. Olga, a short, German blonde, who claimed to be an expert in American crossword puzzles, and Alice, English, with thick glasses, who had lived for years in Alaska with her grown son, liked to talk with him and answered his questions. Sometimes his mother would return just before dinner and tell him that she preferred he go out and play in the afternoon. His brother looked down on him, and although his father tried to guide him his father's advice was useless. He could win over almost all his grammar school teachers—nuns and laywomen—with his manner, dress, and bearing. In the same way, he charmed the mothers of his friends and, when he went with girls, their mothers. He studied phrases in the letters from girls for signs of their true feelings about him: what did it mean when a girl said, "You are important to me"? Sex became so powerful in him that a small attention from a girl meant more to him than the concern of his parents. In high school the Jesuits seemed to like him, but not the lay teachers. His friends among the students were small, poor, and smart; he liked to talk to them about his girls, and they seemed to like to listen. When one of these friendships failed it was unimportant, like an animal's not taking food from him; when a girl dropped him, however, he felt he had done something wrong. In the army he occasionally met an officer who seemed to like him, usually a desk officer, young and a college graduate; noncommissioned officers disliked him: one of them often said he was "on top of the shit list," another that he would do close-order drill "till his shit had muscles." He completed marches, was a good marksman, kept his bunk, uniform, and rifle clean; but after he had been in the army awhile he understood that the job of noncommissioned officers was to get him into a position where he could be killed; he felt they knew he knew that. The year between his discharge and marriage he frequently asked his fiancée if she loved him; she almost always said she did. For the first few years of marriage he thought his wife loved him; but when she began denying him sex he thought she didn't, not because she didn't enjoy the sex but because she didn't want to please him. The woman he had his first adulterous affair with cared about his well-being to the extent that it served her interests, and he valued this to the extent that it served his. His second mistress was a beautiful younger married woman who affected simplicity and was simple, claimed to be selfish and manipulative in certain ways and was in others. She said that as a girl she sometimes exposed a strand of pubic hair from the crotch of her bathing suit. "It drove the boys wild," she said. By not sleeping with him she tried to force him to do certain things, but since what he wanted was a desirous woman he lost interest in her when she did this. His third mistress said that sex with him was better than it had been with anyone and that she trusted him more than she had anyone, but she had had so many disappointments in her life the compliments were not convincing. The fourth approved of everything about him that kept them together; she gave him expensive presents and cultivated his daughters; eventually the attention irritated him as his mother's had. He could not be sure of the feelings of these women, because he felt they were looking for new husbands. Then he finally fell in love with a young woman who seemed to be happily married; after he had taken her away from her husband it occurred to him that it might have been this that had enabled him to fall in love. Later, when they began to argue, he claimed that she couldn't have been happily married: happy marriages can't be broken up. One day when he expressed this idea to the young woman's mother the mother said, "But you told her she was the most beautiful woman you had ever seen." He now holds to a theory of romantic love in which the lover hopes to satisfy some extrasexual desire, like the desire for money, social preferment, or a sense of one's worth. The lover is not conscious of this desire, so that it mixes with sex and becomes obsessive. If the lover's hidden desire is frustrated he seeks greater satisfaction from sex; if this fails, love dies. He could not discern what his own hidden desires had been. In later years he will conclude that success in love is like success in anything, not available to those who don't know what's possible.

His FATHER stopped boxing with him when he was five. Till then he had often stood between his father's knees, throwing punches while his father, sitting on the edge of a chair, feinted and parried, occasionally taking one of his small fists in the face. When he asked his father why he didn't box with him any more his father said that he was getting too big. His father gave the same reason for not playing pickaback or lifting him upside-down by the feet. He thought there was another reason, but he did not know what it was. He and his friends fought with their fists to settle grudges or respond to serious insults. Lesser differences were settled by wrestling. Wrestling established the fighting hierarchy of the group. His own position was high: no one younger than he could beat him, and he could beat a number of older boys. His greatest victory came at thirteen, over his brother, who was twenty. He fixed a cup of water on the frame of his bedroom transom in such a way that when the door was opened the cup would spill. He then went to his brother's room, where his brother was studying, and pounded on the door, a traditional act of incitement. He heard his brother rise; noisily he raced toward his room but hid in a nearby closet. His brother entered the room, and the cup tipped. He had never seen his brother so angry. They wrestled for a long time. Finally he pinned his brother to the floor. He later ascribed his victory to the fact that he had been wearing his Boy Scout uniform. During his first week of college the gym instructor, who was also the wrestling coach, chose him to demonstrate various holds. He resisted one of the holds, the instructor pressed, still he resisted, and soon they were wrestling. He threw the instructor in what the instructor later explained to the class was an unorthodox manner. After the class the instructor invited him to join the wrestling team. He won his first three matches, although he had not mastered basic wrestling techniques. His fourth match was against a blind student. He had no will to win, was pinned in record time, and the next day quit the team. In the army he called a Southern soldier a cracker. The soldier challenged him to a fight. The entire company gathered to watch, splitting into two factions, city boys and country boys. He wrestled while the other soldier boxed. Bleeding at the nose and mouth, he established himself on the soldier's chest and was proclaimed winner. The soldier got to his feet and challenged him to duel with mounted bayonets. He declined, and the soldier's faction proclaimed their man the moral victor. His distaste for army training rid him of any desire for physical contact for years afterward. However, now and then he arm-wrestles and feels a surge of pleasure at male contact. Before long an old friend who had wrestled with him in college will suggest at a party that they give an exhibition. He and the friend will be drunk, and although he will not want to wrestle he will agree because his friend's wife will be present and he will have been thinking of initiating an affair with her. At another party, given by an opera singer, a heavy basso some years younger than he, he will suddenly feel very strong and challenge the singer to Indian-wrestle. The singer will grin, assume the proper position, and with wrist alone bring him to his knees. This will be his first indication that he is weakening with age. He will frequently have contests of strength with women in bed, usually trials of restraint and escape. One evening when he is in his mid-fifties he will be making love to a woman fifteen years younger than he; they will struggle to see who can mount the other. He will be startled and amused at her relative strength, and although he will win he will wonder if other women had falsified their strength to please him. One day when he is parking his car he will pull in front of a Cadillac that had been there before him. The Cadillac owner will blow his horn in protest, get out of his car, grasp him by the lapel, and raise a fist. He will be transfixed by a gold ring on the Cadillac owner's little finger, then look at the man's face and see the anger change to shame because he is too old to be threatened.

After seeing a movie about entering the forbidden tomb of a pharaoh, he wanted to be an Egyptologist. Next he wanted to be an astronomer. Searching the sky for stars alone at night through a telescope was a job he felt he could not fail at. His third ambition was chemistry. Each Christmas he received a progressively more elaborate chemistry set. Just as he was about to get the last one, which came in a hinged, wooden box and cost twenty-five dollars, he began collecting chemicals piecemeal from druggists. Because of his youth most druggists would not sell him poisons or corrosive acids, but he finally found a sympathetic druggist who would even order for him chemicals not in stock. From sulphur, charcoal, and potassium nitrate he made gunpowder, with which he lit bright fires on his window sill and in his bathtub. He then made nitro-cellulose, a relatively powerful explosive, which he packed into glass tubes and when his parents weren't home detonated with paper fuses. He bought a book on explosives, which explained how to make nitroglyc-erine, and although he had the necessary ingredients and equipment he lost his nerve because of a warning in the book that nitroglycerine goes off by itself if im-pure. His favorite experiment, which he performed for friends, was a demonstration of spontaneous combus-tion. He would pour a few drops of glycerine onto a mound of potassium permanganate, and within a min-ute or two the mixture would smoke and burst into flames. One evening when his parents were sitting in the living room he put the glycerine and potassium permanganate into a small screw-top bottle, locked the bottle in a steel box, put the box close to his parents, warning them not to touch it, that it would soon ex-plode. It did, the box hopping a few inches off the floor. His father was angry but said only not to pull that little trick again. Shortly afterward he put potassium per-manganate and glycerine into a corked test tube and dropped the tube onto the awning of the grocery store two floors below his room. The awning caught fire, and he was seen by the grocer trying to extinguish the fire by pouring pans of water from his window. That evening his father wrapped up all his chemicals to dispose of on the dumb-waiter next morning. He rose at dawn, undid his father's package, and salvaged his most prized chemical, an ounce of mercury, which he liked to manipulate on a flat surface, watching it break into tiny balls and recombine into larger masses. In the last two years of grammar school he delivered oratorical pieces and performed in plays for the parents of students. He got so much credit for this that he searched out collections of poems and prose passages intended for recitation. Learning and saying these gave him a sense of verbal harmony. In his third year of high school he wrote a realistic description of his fellow students, how they smelled bad, squeezed pimples, masturbated; the composition was a great success. Also, for a girl he had fallen in love with he wrote poems, which she said she treasured. By the end of high school he had decided to be a writer. When he told his father that this was his ambition his father said that he would have to pick something more practical if he wanted to be sent to college. He lied and said in that case he would be a teacher. For a time he considered being a photographer but realized that his gratification came from unflattering pictures he took of relatives and friends (he even used special darkroom techniques to deform pleasant portraits). He had no success as a writer until he wrote comic stories about his marital difficulties. They seemed to be even-handed caricatures of his wife and himself;

his wife, however, understood that she was being represented as an inadequate woman and he as her victim.
While he was writing his first novel he suspected that
for him the point of literary composition was vengeance
and an extension of his childhood interest in explosives.
Some years after the end of his marriage he fell in love.
The experience so loosened his feelings that he hoped
to write warmly of people, but he still has pity only for
himself and a strong sense of grievance against others.
Eventually he will understand that most people have as
hard a time in life as he. He will try to make literature
from this understanding, but he will not be able to.

After he was expelled from private school he went to public school, where he was encouraged to take part in an extracurricular activity. He chose dramatics and was cast as the hero in the current production. Alec, who had an amusing face and voice and was playing a comic role, took him up. He liked Alec but not in the way Alec liked him. Alec mythicized him, made much of the stories and poems he was writing, and represented him to friends as a genius. He felt that he was being overvalued, but this stimulated his wit, which in turn stimulated Alec's crush. After high school Alec went to a second-rate college, he to a first-rate college. In a year they both entered the army. Alec was sent to a combat outfit, he to a language school. After the war Alec told him that many times he had almost been killed. Once on the front a sergeant had gone from foxhole to foxhole seeking volunteers for a dangerous mission. Alec refused. The sergeant said he hadn't expected anything else from a Jew. Alec told the sergeant that he was refusing because he was a coward, not because he was a Jew. After six months of steady combat Alec was removed to a rest area. Alec on his own initiative went to a psychiatrist and said he couldn't take any more combat. The psychiatrist reassigned Alec to the military police. The psychiatrist was a Jew, and the next day Alec returned to thank the psychiatrist and say that he too was a Jew. The psychiatrist said that had he known this he would have sent Alec back into combat: Our people have a special duty in this war, the psychiatrist said. Alec married a bright, small girl who whispered, wrote poetry, and drew pictures. She often spoke paradoxically, after which she would smile and squint. She and Alec were protective of one another, which made him jealous because his own wife, he felt, was becoming an enemy. One evening when the four of them were together Alec's wife suggested that they swap mates for the night. Alec, Alec's wife, and he agreed; his wife refused, saying that she took the marriage vows seriously. As he and his wife were leaving, Alec's wife whispered to him that perhaps love affairs should be arranged by twos, not fours. A week later, after reserving a room at a motel, he met Alec's wife in a parking lot near her house. Sitting in her car, he asked her where Alec thought she was. "With you," she said. He excused himself and went home. Alec at the time was making four times his salary and offered him a job at a good wage. He found it impossible to be friends with Alec after this. His marriage and Alec's broke up at the same time. They both moved out of their homes, he to a friend's vacated apartment, Alec to a hotel, where a month later Alec died in a fire that had started in Alec's room. He began seeing a psychiatrist and in the spirit of therapy invited Alec's widow to lunch with him at his apartment on Tuesdays. He fed her, gave her wine, and let her talk, interrupting every now and then with advice. He made love to her on two successive Tuesdays; on the third he said that they should not do this any more. "I understand," she said; "because of Alec." He nodded. Soon after, the meetings stopped; but she often invited him to lunch or dinner. He was upset by the strangeness of her adolescent children, two pretty girls who affected odd clothes and hair styles and used hallucinogenic drugs. Alec's widow now has a young lover, with whom she does creative things. She makes videotapes of original musical plays, in which her daughters are actors. Everything she creates deals with the theme of the interchangeability of the concepts of sanity and insanity. Her home will become a refuge for disturbed people, whom she will counsel. She will send him copies of her creations: tapes, Xeroxed drawings, privately printed books. She will inquire about his state of mind, and he will invent troubles to tell her. She will offer to cure him with new methods of meditation, yoga-like exercises, and her special insights into the problems of the human condition. Eventually he will try to avoid her. He will hear from a friend that she and one of her daughters have gone to South America to live. The most that he will be able to make of all this is that life was better to him than to Alec.

ONE CHRISTMAS an aunt gave him a two-and-a-half-dollar gold piece, a coin smaller than a dime. His mother was afraid he would lose it and had it changed at the bank into pennies. He enjoyed the pennies, piling them into stacks, which represented castles, and attacking them with marbles, which represented armies. When he tired of the pennies he asked his mother to change them into nickels. He liked the solidity and dull luster of nickels, much preferring the Indian heads, with the big nose and feathers, to the virtuous profile on the Liberty heads. Eventually he had the nickels changed into twenty-five dimes, which he spent. Four times a year his father traveled to the West Coast and brought back a silver dollar each for him and his brother. When he had collected five or six he spent them; since silver dollars were minted and used mainly in the West, store clerks and movie cashiers sometimes called on superiors to authenticate them. The summer he was eight he asked his mother for a weekly allowance beyond the nightly nickel he was given for ice cream or candy. Fifteen cents was decided on, and his mother said it would be a good thing if he saved it but that under no circumstances should he spend it all at once. With his first allowance, however, and the night's nickel he bought a Coke, a cone, a Mary Jane, and a frozen Milky Way and vomited outside the soda fountain. In the city on schoolday mornings his mother gave him five cents, which he spent on his way home for lunch: three cents for the newspaper and two for an unwrapped chocolate bar with nuts. His closest grammar school friend never had money, but they parted before the candy store so there was no embarrassment. He seemed to have more money than his contemporaries. In high school he was able with the money his mother gave him for carfare and incidentals to treat any boy he chose to a hamburger and coffee after school at a favorite counter that advertised hamburgers "with a college education"; this was during the depression, and the twelve cents one cost was expensive. In the army he made fifty dollars a month; it was gone in two weeks. To keep in cigarettes and beer he and his friends would, one by one, hock their watches in town for ten or fifteen dollars apiece, then redeem them on the first pass after payday. The last possession to go—just before payday—was his best friend's lucky silver dollar. He and the friend would tell a sympathetic woman clerk at the PX that they were broke: could they use the lucky silver dollar to buy beer and retrieve it in a day or two? Many of the PX women were married to servicemen overseas and soft on soldiers' needs; most agreed. When he married, his father gave him a thousand dollars, more money than he had had before; he resisted spending it, feeling that it should be kept intact as if it weren't his. However, it slipped away without pleasure on everyday items. One evening he took his wife and a couple to a night club for dinner; when the check came he removed from his inside pocket an alligator wallet and from the wallet took a wad of newsprint sheets cut like old-fashioned five-pound notes. Ceremoniously he unfolded them as he had seen done many times in British movies. He placed three sheets on the check, and returned the rest to his wallet and the wallet to his jacket. His wife and friends got the joke, but the waiter called the manager, who stood by the table until the bill was paid with green American money. Although his wife worked and between them they should have had enough money to live comfortably, she came from a poor family in which anyone who saved was penalized by having the savings called upon at the first family crisis. Because of this and the problems between them they could not save, even for things they agreed they wanted, but spent in reciprocal hostility. When he left his family he accepted a punishing settlement and lived on windfalls. For two weeks he worked at night on a movie script for a foreign director; to avoid taxes he was paid in cash, with three five-hundred-dollar bills. He took the director to lunch and put one of the bills on the check; they watched the waiter do a double take; the waiter said, "I've seen these before." Now that his children are grown and his former wife has renounced her alimony he feels well off. He brings pennies into the house but does not take them out; he has a large salad bowl full of pennies, which he likes to dig his fingers into and show to friends. He intends to give them someday to a child visitor. He has lost his regard for quarters and dimes now that they are copper-filled and ring false. As prices continue to rise year after year he feels uneasy about keeping money, although he will keep it, just as when he was young he felt uneasy about spending money, although he spent it.

His MOTHER went to the door to kiss his father when his father came home from work. Sometimes his mother would comment that his father had had a drink; his father would agree and explain that he had stopped off with a few of the men on the way from the office. His mother did not drink; she claimed it gave her palpitations. He liked the smell of liquor on his father's breath but on no one else's. The bungalows of their summer community were close together; some of the childless couples drank on weekends, visited back and forth late into the night, and occasionally had playful fights with carbonated water. One summer his parents brought a woman from the city to help with the housework; the first day the woman finished off the gin (filling the bottle with water, his father later discovered), and the next day she was sent back to the city. He and a friend sold cold canned beer to men who came from the city to fish along the shore. One day he and the friend were left with ten unsold cans, which they drank rather than carry back. They giggled, fell on the sand, stumbled in and out of the water, and later agreed that they had had a good time. In the second year of high school he and some other students took to going to a rathskeller in the afternoon; they lied about their ages, drank Tom Collinses, and discussed the seduction of the owner's two pink-faced daughters, who waited on table in peasant costume and seemed more available as the afternoons progressed. One weekend when his family was at the beach he finished two thirds of a fifth of whiskey, not getting drunk, but nipping away, listening to the radio, napping, writing poetry and letters. Monday his mother saw the empty bottle and, weeping, pleaded with him not to drink; her father had died from drink, she said. (Years later she told him that her father had left the family one day and not come back.) Some nights he would come home drunk from dates, and if his parents were awake he would stand for a moment at the door of their room to report bits of the evening. Once he asked his mother if she had noticed that he had been drunk on these occasions, and she said no. When he was in the army he brought back from a three-day pass a bottle of peach brandy, which, since he slept on the top bunk, he could hide on the shelf behind his pillow. Each morning till the bottle was gone he took a swig, which improved the day's first hour, one of the worst. He considered turning himself into an alcoholic to get a discharge (preferable to faking homosexuality, the most commonly discussed way) but doubted he could get the liquor. He wrote his first novel on beer, drinking one can after another until the writing became confused, usually on the third page, between the fourth and fifth can. When he left his family he drank a lot; mornings-after, the evenings seemed to have slipped by without thought or incident. One morning after having been at a drunken party he saw that his car was damaged: the convertible top was torn, the hood was dented, and a piece of wood stuck out from behind the bumper. At first he thought that the damage had been done during the night while the car was parked on the street, then he vaguely remembered having driven through an unattended police barrier on a highway; as he recalled the details he realized that the obstacle might as well have been a stone wall, and he gave up drunken driving for a while. He worries about his drinking, and brings it up with his doctor, who feels his liver and says that if he thinks he is drinking too much by all means cut down. As he gets older he will drink less, to compensate, he says, for his decreasing mental agility. Actually drinking will give him heartburn, and he will develop a fear that if he drinks he may vomit in his sleep and choke to death.

PROTESTANT CHILDREN were different from Catholic and Jewish children: Protestant children didn't talk about what went on in their homes, had few visitors, didn't have to be doing something all the time, and got along with their families; Protestant parents smiled but were not friendly. He liked Protestant children but did not get so close to them as to Catholic and Jewish children. Although he lived in a Jewish neighborhood there were few Jews in his apartment house; this, he thought, was because his house had a garden and no elevators. He knew that the Jewish children were Jewish but did not bring the subject up with them or they with him. No one objected to phrases like "Jew down" for getting a lower price or "Jew Boy's" for a local candy store run by a stupid birdlike man with an accent. His best city friend said one day, "I guess I'm Jewish, my mother's Jewish"; he then thought he knew why there was always the smell of cooking in the friend's apartment. His father and his father's family were Protestant and glum; his father's brothers and sisters never had money, were too proud to take menial jobs, and more or less lived off his father. When he was expelled from Catholic high school and went to public school all the friends he made there were Jewish. He found this out gradually: for instance, he went with one friend to another friend's house, where he saw Hebrew books. He later asked the first friend whether the second friend was Jewish. "Yes, and I am too," the first friend said. When this happened the friends did not have to be taken so seriously and their virtues were partially discounted because he thought Jews worked hard at developing themselves, whereas he kept discovering hidden talents in Catholics. More and more of his friends were Jewish; he told them everything about himself, and they seemed to tell him everything about themselves. They were knowing, bookish, funny, and admiring of him while inwardly he could be condescending to them. To meet a Jew in the army was a great treat, especially if the Jew came from a big city. His closest friend at one post was a tall, thin, small-headed, thick-lipped Jew; one night while drinking beer with the friend at a picnic table behind a PX two country soldiers exchanged loud anti-Semitic clichés. He seemed more upset than the friend and said to the friend that he thought Jews were warm-hearted, open, and intelligent people, which he believed but later realized were also clichés. He had never heard anti-Catholic sentiments until once after the war at a bar a Protestant student told him about wanting to get married, "but my mother keeps breaking it up." One of this student's romances had been with a Catholic girl, "but Mother was right about that one, I would have been a fool to get mixed up with that Catholic business." "Like what?" he asked. "Oh, you know," the student said, but at the time he didn't. A few years after his father died he, his brother, and his mother were having lunch at a restaurant, as they did every month, and his brother told of having sent to the United States Archives for their paternal grandfather's Civil War records, which told how the grandfather had been AWOL for two weeks, lost an Austrian rifle, and been docked pay for the offenses. "Also there was something that would interest you," his brother said. "In the form he filled out for a pension he gave his mother's maiden name, place of birth, and occupation. It was Caroline Isaacs, London, milliner. Your grandfather was a Jew or half a Jew." They asked their mother for more information; she said, "Well, Daddy and I knew something about it, but we never said." That evening he called an expert in Jewish things to ask how he would have fared in Germany in the thirties. The expert said, "A fourth you were a Jew, a sixteenth you were not, an eighth it depended on whether you played ball." He told his daughters they were probably part Jewish; they told their friends, some of whom threw a party with Jewish food and wine. It then occurred to him that the only anti-Semitism he had heard at home had come from his father, who had worked resentfully for a Jewish company and had not gotten along with the presumably Jewish or half-Jewish grandfather. He thinks that Jews want to remain inwardly different from gentiles while becoming outwardly similar, thus increasing advantage; that Protestants want to be good without forgoing the things of this world; and that Catholics want to believe that the world can be changed, thus relieving themselves of the urge for self-improvement. As he ages he will notice that his contemporaries mix more with their own kind and seem to be glad to be done with outsiders. This will not be so easy for him because his own kind will be a kind of outsider; but he will seek them out because he will enjoy talking about childhood and youth and will want to be readily understood; the other parts of life, he will feel, were discussed enough while being lived.

ONE EVENING his father told a funny story about a friend who had tried and couldn't learn to play the kazoo. His father wasn't often funny and when requested would retell this story. Occasionally his father took him to lunch with business acquaintances; his father laughed more among them than at home. When he told his mother a joke she would say it was funny but not laugh. It was easy to get a smile from her because she was pleased with him; from his father it was easy to get a laugh because his father was surprised when he did or said something amusing. In school it was satisfying to make another student laugh so that the student would be reprimanded by the teacher; this could be done by a well-timed comment or grimace, or by goosing a student standing to recite. He had a repertory of jokes and was asked to tell them over and over. The favorite concerned an American visitor to England to whom it was explained that in England a man sitting in the first row of a theater balcony was permitted to piss into the orchestra; when the American did this a voice from below was heard: "Would you mind wobbling it a bit? I'm getting it all, you know." He could make friends laugh without jokes: by tensing his body and simulating a fit; by putting a lit cigarette into his ear and exhaling smoke he had held in his mouth; if a girl was present, by opening his fly and pulling out a shirttail. Once when eating a ham sandwich in a cafeteria with his friend Alec he pressed the far side of the sandwich as he was about to bite the near side. The near side opened like a mouth. He closed his mouth, the sandwich closed. He continued the routine, and people laughed for tables around. Once when he was clowning among friends a newcomer to the neighborhood called him a fool; later the death of the boy in the war made sense to him. When he was courting the girl he would marry he could make her and her sisters laugh at will and would amuse them for hours in the kitchen after their parents had gone to bed. When he was first married he continued to be able to make his wife laugh, with a funny face, an obscene gesture, putting on a piece of her clothing; after their first child was born, however, laughs were harder to get; finally they came only by chance. When his children were babies he could make them laugh by suddenly disappearing, then reappearing. When they could talk he would challenge one of them to keep a straight face after he had said a special word. Often the child would laugh waiting for the word. The word or phrase that never failed was *belly button;* part of the game would be for the child to guess whether he would say belly button or not. Once when he was playing the game with the younger child the older, who had become resistant to it, challenged him to keep a straight face for her word. The word was poppycock, which he laughed at out of politeness but which shocked him. Once when his wife caught him surreptitiously talking with a girl on the phone and laughing she said, "What kind of a marriage is this where I get all your tears and someone else gets all your laughter?"; and when she discovered that he was sleeping with another woman she said, "I don't mind the sex you two have together, I mind the laughing." Years later, after he had fallen in love and he and the woman were laughing at a bar while waiting for curtain time a drunk told them it would never work, they were having too much fun. He could not make this woman laugh when he wanted to; when he told her a joke she grunted. Sometimes she would become amused at her own thoughts and laugh for a long time without telling him what was funny. It seems to him that people do not laugh so much as they used to. Occasionally when he and friends smoke marijuana together they laugh like children. After his mother becomes senile he will be able to make her laugh by entering into her confusion. For instance, she will say, "I saw two dogs in the doorway today," an impossibility. He will ask, "A light one and a dark one?" "I think so," she will say. "Were their names . . . ?" and he will say the names of his ex-wife and his sister-in-law. His mother will look wary for a few seconds, then get the joke and laugh. As he becomes older he will think that fewer things are funny to him because he understands more things.

IN THE SUMMER he stayed out at night till the lights went on along the walk. He felt that if his parents had allowed it he would have stayed out all night and slept on the beach or at a friend's house. He didn't like getting into bed; it meant the fun was over. In his house a person sleeping in the day was not awakened except for meals. His mother often said, "Anyone who falls asleep needs a sleep." The summer he was thirteen a friend arranged a date with two girls he didn't know. The plan was for him and the friend to meet the girls on the girls' beach, four miles away. The night of the date he went to bed in a bathing suit. The friend scratched on the screen at midnight and he climbed out of the window. They waited at the side of the bunga-low to see that they had not awakened anyone, then walked and trotted the four miles along the shore to the girls' beach. His girl was prettier than his friend's girl. There was a full moon, and the couples separated. He and his girl watched the phosphorescence in the water, and she told him that her favorite book was Robert Nathan's *Portrait of Jennie*. They agreed to meet eight years hence on her twenty-first birthday at 8 p.m. in the lobby of a certain midtown hotel, and they kissed on it. On the way home he asked his friend why the friend had arranged for him to have the prettier girl. "Mine jerked me off," the friend said. He was in the army on the girl's twenty-first birthday. When marching or training, the soldiers had a ten-minute break every hour; he usually slept through the ten minutes, lying down and falling asleep with his pack on as soon as the whistle blew, and waking when it blew again. His wife often woke him for trivial reasons when he was sleeping in the day: to ask a question or make a comment. She slept so deeply he sometimes could not wake her even by sitting her upright and whistling in her ear; he envied her until he realized that probably she had developed the ability against the noisy household of her childhood. In his thirties he heard from a friend that the girl he had met on the beach at night remembered him and on learning that he had published a book said, "I knew it: I should have held on to that one." Presumably she was unsatisfactorily married, and he thought of looking her up but didn't. He also heard that the friend who had arranged the date was dead, having had a stroke and on subsequent examination been found to be "riddled with cancer." Shortly afterward he became afraid that he was going to die; and he would come home from his office after work, eat dinner, and sleep for fourteen hours. Only the first two or three minutes after waking in the morning were free from the fear. This fear enabled him to have his first adulterous affair: not because he had nothing to lose but because sex was the only thing that continued to interest him. One evening he told his mistress that he wanted to take a nap before they dressed to go to their homes, and he slept with his head on her stomach, listening to the sounds of her innards. He woke in a few minutes exalted: his doctor, a homosexual, said that this meant the woman was a friend as well as a mistress. After he left his family his initial sleep at nights was often a drunken stupor, and when he woke from it he would listen to an all-night classical-music station. Once the announcer played Gregorian chants intermixed with readings from Gibbon on Pope Gregory the Great; the announcer was fired soon after for mocking the commercials. When he first slept all night with the woman he had fallen in love with he stayed awake in order not to miss the pleasure of her presence. When they moved in together sleep became a problem: she complained that he woke at night, lay tense, and thereby woke her; or he snored or tossed and thereby woke her. Now he sleeps in another room, about which she also complains. He feels that the difference between sleeping and waking is diminishing: when asleep he is aware that he is asleep, and when awake he often falls into reveries. Up and in company after 10 p.m. he will nod, particularly when drinking. Only once in a while will he sleep through the night; he will never sleep so deeply that he does not know where he is on waking. His dreams will most often be confused extensions of the day's concerns. Near the end of his life, after not dreaming of his father for years, he will have a dream in which his father taunts him for looking old. He will try to take the offensive by pointing out that his father had always looked older than his mother and that usually those who look old for their age die younger than those who look young for their age. He will explain the thought as well as he can, but as he talks his father's face will turn into the face of a self-satisfied rodent.

For comfort he took certain objects with him to school. They had to be simple and impermeable. Ball bearings were almost perfect. The top of his desk tipped toward him, so he would put the ball bearings into the pencil groove. When they were struck together they would make a satisfying sound, but their movement in the groove and their relative positions restricted the ways he could think about them. When he was in the third grade his father gave him a magnifying glass of the kind used by textile merchants; it opened to form three sides of a cube and folded to a flat square. The hinged workings were smooth and tight, and the brushed surface of the stainless-steel frame offered a pleasant resistance to his passing thumb and finger pads. The glass was strong, and when a friend pointed out that, abandoned on a desert island, he could use it to concentrate sunlight and start a fire the object took on extra value. He liked well-made penknives. One day in class he was playing with a penknife that had a bone handle and a scimitar-shaped blade. It closed on his right index finger. He could not open it with his left hand and had to take it to the teacher. She opened the knife and kept it, he felt unjustly. Sometimes he yearned to have a hunting knife in a leather case hidden under his arm or along his calf, but he never acted on the desire. In high school, after composing a poem, he would type it on a sheet of paper, fold the paper in four, and put it into the side pocket of his jacket to take out and read when unobserved, occasionally changing a word or phrase. He would keep the poem with him until he wrote a new one. He gave up knives in high school, and in the army all weapons became repugnant to him. But he took a penknife on his honeymoon, along with a honing stone and a can of oil to slow the action of the stone. At leisure moments he honed the knife to an ever finer edge. When his marriage in its slow dissolution took temporary turns for the better he would buy a new knife to celebrate. When he began adulterous affairs he sometimes marked them by buying a new knife. Often he carried a book with him. At its most powerful the right book, he felt, would save him from death or see him through death without panic or despair.

His favorites were small editions of Herrick, Catullus, Lucretius, and *Antony and Cleopatra*. From a copy of Marvell's poems he cut the page containing "To His Coy Mistress" and for years carried it with him, although he knew the poem by heart. During his long crisis, when he thought he was going to die, he was drawn to his wife's house plants. He would study them before he left the house in the morning and when he returned in the evening. He made cuttings and distributed them to friends and neighbors so that something of the plants was sure to survive. His wife in her separation complaint mentioned the knife on the honeymoon. Recently he understood that the stroking of the knife on a stone represented the thrust of his penis in a vagina; this pleases him because he had thought that the association of knives and women came from fear or hostility. Although he travels with personal equipment—pen, keys, wallet—nothing material has saving significance for him now. Soon he will feel that the quality of immutability, which once attracted him to certain objects, is worthless and that only certain ephemeral qualities, such as those present in the body of an athlete, are reassuring. He will treasure plant seeds for their intricate organization of information and keep them on his desk like talismans.

He was uncircumcised, and the head of his penis was sensitive. He would pull back the foreskin but only so far. Once a doctor pulled it back all the way. This seemed to him a violation, and he made his mother promise not to let the doctor do it again. Once in the bath when he was flicking his penis, small and soft, from side to side in play his mother told him he must not fool with it or he would get sick. At nine he became aware that his penis changed in size and firmness; this struck him as unnatural. On his waking in the morning it was often large and hard and would not soften until he urinated. Urinating was difficult with a hard penis. The stream would shoot off to one side and miss the bowl, or perhaps split into two streams, one or both of which would miss the bowl If the stream went singly—say, to a half-right—and he compensated by pointing the penis to the left the stream might suddenly straighten and miss the bowl on the other side. A sure way to get all the urine into the bowl was to sit down on the toilet and force the hard penis under the rim of the seat. This would be painful if he didn't bend forward, and even then the urine would splash off the enamel, wetting his hands and the penis itself. The first time he saw a vulva he was walking along a neighborhood street in early summer. Children of seven or eight were jumping rope and playing potsy. Suddenly one little girl hiked up her short cotton dress, pulled her panties to one side, and scratched her cunt. It was no more than a small hairless crack, but his face burned for a long time afterward. He didn't touch a cunt until he was twenty, in the army, and about to make love to a whore. After getting into bed with her, he felt around under the sheet for her cunt. He thought it would be in front, like a prick; but it wasn't. He was unwilling to ask the woman for help because he didn't want her to know he was a virgin. He remembered the saying that a nice girl was a girl who put it in for you, and, propping himself over her, he placed her hand on his prick, and she guided it in. He was surprised that the cunt was between a woman's legs, and for some time considered this a fault. Through the first eight years of marriage the only cunt he knew was his wife's. Although he thought about it a lot, was greatly attracted to it, invented fond jokes about it, his wife made it less and less accessible, and he was returned to a state of constant yearning, as in adolescence. He grew to feel that women tolerated rather than desired a prick in their cunts, so that when he had his first adulterous love affair, at thirty, he doubted that his mistress really enjoyed him. One night she convinced him that she did by telling him that he was a cautious fucker and that he should feel free to fuck her as hard as he wanted. His subsequent experiences with other woman made him feel at home with cunts. He would examine them carefully, play with the lips and fatty mons veneris, lick the clitoris and insert his tongue as far as he could into the vagina. Sometimes a cunt had a different character from its owner. Two women he slept with, although desirous, had cunts that seemed to narrow to a wedge and want him out. Another girl, who always looked angry when he fucked her, had a cunt that held his prick like a treasure. Occasionally a cunt was too large for friction. He solved the problem with one girl by squeezing the bottom of her ass with his hand when he made love to her. Now cunts are less important in themselves; he values them mainly as a means of attaching women to him. Through their cunts he makes women like and need him, and this does much to compensate for his growing coldness toward the world.

Most of the cunts he knows in his fifties belong to women in their forties. As he ages, so will the women he sleeps with. In his late fifties he will yearn for the cunt of a girl. He will try to imagine it—round, small, firm, with a full springy bush. Sometimes this will increase his pleasure when he is sleeping with older women and sometimes lessen it. He will pick up a young whore one night, the second and last whore of his life; but a Caesarian scar and her contemptuous manner will make copulation perfunctory. Near the end of his life he will develop a feeling for his penis akin to the faint fondness he felt for it when he was a child, that is, before the onset of the dilemmas and frustrations of adolescence. Except for odd, recollective moments and occasionally in dreams he will lose his attraction for cunts, and when he makes love he will hardly think of them.

HE AND THE OTHER BOYS were told not to be rough with girls, girls were built differently and were easily injured. Girls had long hair, which put them at a disadvantage in games and fights. In the city, he stopped playing with girls when he became bigger and stronger than girls his age. For a while some of the girls tried to stay equal with boys by fighting with them and taking dares, but the girls lost the fights and failed the dares; also, girls wept without shame. Soon the boys and girls hardly greeted one another. They never got together again, because when they started dating they went outside the neighborhood for partners. In his summer community, however, the boys and girls played together until they were thirteen or fourteen and then paired off. At the beach girls could fall on sand or in the water without getting hurt; girls swam as fast as some boys; the games were mostly word, board, and card games, at which girls were as good as boys; and because there was more room, leisure, and pleasure than in the city there was less fighting. When he was twelve girls began wearing playsuits, one-piece cotton garments with short pants and overall tops. Standing beside a girl in a playsuit as she pitched horseshoes, he sometimes could see the edge of her breast; there were no such delights in the city. One evening in the city when he was fifteen and had given up fighting he playfully insulted a thirteen-year-old girl in her parents' apartment. She slapped him; automatically he hit her face with the flat of his hand and knocked her to the floor. As he helped her up he was surprised at how small she was and realized that except for dancing and light necking he had not touched a girl for years. When he was on the wrestling team the coach asked him and the one-hundred-and-seventy-pound varsity wrestler to take on together the varsity heavyweight, who was national champion and had no effective opponents to practice with. The heavyweight picked them up, one under each arm, knelt down, and pressed their backs to the mat. His wife was tall and thin like him and for a time seemed a perfect mate in bed. When he began having love affairs some of the women were small; always when seeing such a woman naked for the first time she seemed like a child, unlikely to be able to bear his weight and thrust, whereas before seeing her naked she had seemed his physical equal. He was used to feeling bigger than most people, and once when talking to a very tall man he stood on a chair in a compulsive joke to complete the conversation. After he left his family he lived in a small apartment with frail furniture. The apartment was burgled; two burly policemen came to investigate; they seemed bull-like in the place, where he had been entertaining, he realized, only women and small men. The policemen addressed him by his first name; he felt they thought he was homosexual. The woman he finally fell in love with was broad-hipped, broad-shouldered, and fleshy. He had not touched a body like hers since dancing as an adolescent, when fleshiness put him off. He liked her to lie on him, which she would do but then not, saying that it made her feel like a dinosaur. Occasionally he dreams of her as a South American Indian statue, imposing and implacable, but with short, feckless arms. When she leaves him he will sleep with women of various sizes, and sometimes when lying at rest after intercourse, his hand on the woman's back, he will feel the same satisfying deep flesh but will not like the woman's color, smell, movements, or some other quality that in the woman he had loved was perfect. One day soon before his mother's death he will find her fallen in a faint on her bedroom floor. She will have soiled herself; he will clean her while waiting for the doctor and think how inapplicable to him the Oedipus complex is. When he is too old to trust to sexual encounters—not from inability, he feels, but from fear of offending a partner's sensibilities—he will understand that nothing had been so beautiful and ugly to him as human bodies.

HE STUDIED THE OLDER BOYS and admired those he thought were handsome, helpful, and modest. He hoped to be like them, but when the time came he wasn't. He was not picked for class office or team leadership (at best he was chosen spokesman: say, to deliver a complaint to a storekeeper or be prosecutor in a class trial). When someone fair and authoritative was needed it turned out to be one of the even-featured and thoughtful-looking boys, who were slow to speak and laugh, who let younger boys play in games, and who were listened to by adults. When he began to be attracted to girls, he liked those who had the same serene and selfless faces he had admired in the boys. He looked for kindness, stability, and understanding in a girl's face; prominent bones meant long-lastingness, large eyes honesty, clear skin clear-headedness and loyalty. His first girl friend among his summer friends had a perfect face; actually, she was secretive and moody; and it wasn't until years later, when he looked her up, that her face had changed to fit her character. The girl he married had an open, delicate, boyish face; and on account of it he thought she would be the perfect companion for him. When he was introduced to the woman he would have his first adulterous affair with he didn't like her looks or manner: she was slight and soft, had an almond-shaped face, and spoke piercingly, wittily, and condescendingly. In their year and a half together they made love every Wednesday—ass Wednesday, they called it—and although her face became precious to him it did not fit the early model: this may have kept him from feeling that he loved her. One evening at a party he had gone to alone he met a sharp-and-goofy-looking woman from Ohio. He took her home, and they necked until dawn. Through her clothes she let him play with her genitals, but she would not let him touch her breasts, which when she finally was about to undress she said were small. She told him that she was divorced and that she had denounced her husband, a college teacher, to the school administration as a homosexual, although, he discovered, she based this judgment of her husband on the husband's inability to make love to her. They made love once a week for a few months.

One evening she asked him to put off his orgasm, and he fucked her for an hour. She asked him to withdraw so they could switch around on the bed, then wouldn't let him re-enter. He was so angry he wrecked his car on the way home. He didn't see her again; but her once-comic looks—long face and nose, buck teeth, target-centered eyes—came to seem ominous in recollection. A colleague invited him on a blind date to meet two girls, one of whom was the colleague's mistress and the other the mistress's friend. The friend had a plain face and an ordinary mind. At the end of the evening she promised to go to bed with him on their next date. He asked her to lunch the following day and said he thought they should quit, one of them would get hurt. "Which one?" she said. "You," he said. "Let me take care of myself," she said, so they began going to bed. He visited her one Saturday morning because it was her birthday, brought flowers, and fucked her all day, intending to compensate in quantity for what was wanting in quality. Although he had two showers her perfume stayed on him, and he vomited and shat all night; by morning he had lost ten pounds and understood that he had a taboo against sleeping with a woman he liked nothing about. He slept with a young married woman he had known since she was a child. She had the most beautiful face he had ever seen, and while making love to her he would raise his body to watch her. She was used to compliments, and he did not feel he could make her understand how beautiful she was to him. She was concerned only with commonplace things; still he could listen to her for hours on the phone because her voice evoked her face. Sometimes they would masturbate together over the phone: "All right," he would say, "let's synchronize our crotches." The woman he finally fell in love with after leaving his wife had a strong face, from her mother, but unmarked by experience; the mother's face showed that life had been better to her than she had expected it to be. The daughter is full of anger, which shows on her face frequently but leaves no traces; nor will it so long as he knows her. His own mother will look cheery till a year before her death, when her eyes will roll and look inward, her forehead be full of crosses; her nose and ears seem to grow; and her upper lip and chin turn brown at times like a muzzle.

His BROTHER resembled his mother. He resembled his father. At first he thought his father was handsome. Later he thought his father was ugly and hoped he would grow up to look like someone else. He had a fat face and wished it were lean. He thought his mouth was soft and, examining himself in the mirror, often clenched his teeth and narrowed his lips. He wanted to look hard, and outdoors he adopted a severe manner. In adolescence he was pleased to hear that this or that girl liked his looks, but he doubted the girl's taste. When he went into the army he was told to get a short haircut; he had his head shaved instead and felt very manly. When the army sent him far from home his face, chest, and back broke out in lumps. An army doctor said that nothing could be done about the condition because it was only disfiguring, not disabling. After he returned from one furlough his company commander, a man with dark, smooth skin, showed him a red-bordered letter from Eleanor Roosevelt. It told how his mother had written to Mrs. Roosevelt complaining that the army had not given him proper medical care. He was sent to the camp dermatologist, who insisted, despite his denials, that the lumps had been there since he was thirteen or fourteen. At another camp he went to a dermatologist, who reassigned him to limited service, which he afterwards thought might have saved his life. By the time he was discharged from the army his face was scarred. He was grateful to his girl friend for still caring about him and a year later married her. Occasionally she caressed the scars, and although her touch was soothing it embarrassed him. For years he considered the scars not part of himself; in dreams his face was as smooth as when he was a boy. He envied men with good skin. Once when getting off a ferry he offered to help a scarred young woman carry her heavy bag. She refused; he was relieved but thought that they had lost a chance for comfort. He had his first adulterous affair with a woman who said his scars made him look dangerous, although later she said that his constant concern with his appearance was faggy. Later another woman he was sleeping with said that without the scars he would have been too handsome for comfort. Because of his successes with women he now accepts the face he sees in the mirror as his own. As time goes on, the scars will be absorbed, even to the extent that unscarred skin on one side of his face will change as if to re-establish symmetry with scarred skin on the other side. For a while he will be amused by the signs of age: lines in his cheeks and between his eyebrows, ridges in his fingernails, spots on the backs of his hands, yellowing teeth, hair falling from his head and growing in his ears ("just nature moving things around," he will say). But he will be put off by other, later signs: the boniness of knees and elbows, a breakdown of the orderly retreat of his hairline, the pendulousness of his earlobes, a whiteness to the skin of his inner arms, a looseness around the eyes so that they do not express his moods. He will have hoped to age into a rosy cragginess, but instead there will be a general slackness and grayness. When he understands that all future changes will be for the worse he will be struck by the fact that never in his life will he have been satisfied with his appearance. More and more he will remind himself of his father as he remembers his father before his father died. At night when he wakes and coughs or clears his throat he will hear his father's sounds. In unexpected reflections in shop windows he will see his father's late face: irritable, confused, and suspicious. Somewhere among his belongings he will know there are photographs of his father as an old man, which he will intend to search out and study in order to discern how close the resemblance is. If the resemblance is an illusion it will mean to him that his life span is not determined by the genes of his father, who died at seventy-two, but may be modified by those of his mother, who will have lived longer.

He and his brother slept in the same room in separate beds. His brother was seven years older than he and went to bed later. Sometimes he was awake when his brother came in, and they joked. If he woke in the night his brother would be there. When he was six and his brother was about to begin high school his parents decided that his brother needed a room to himself to study in. The family moved to a larger apartment. He did not like sleeping alone. To be happy he had to be with a friend and the friend had to do what he wanted. If a friend would not do what he wanted he was disappointed but not so much that he preferred to be alone. His best city friend from the time he was two till he went into the army was a year younger than he, not so smart as he, weaker, and did almost everything he wanted. On Sunday afternoons they walked across a bridge over a river. One cold Sunday their noses ran. They wiped them on their sleeves until there were no dry spots left. Then they wiped them on the iron railing of the bridge and laughed so they couldn't walk until they separated. (After the war, when he had gotten his first job, his friend told him that when they were children the friend imagined that he would grow up to be a janitor; this surprised him because he thought he had been a hero to the friend.) When he became interested in girls he didn't mind solitude so much. He often sat for hours in his room reading, writing, or thinking. He read plays so that someday he could become a playwright and meet Katharine Hepburn; he wrote poems and letters to the girl he liked at the moment; and he thought a lot about the future: what he would look like when he was a man, where he would live and travel, what it would be like to be married or have love affairs. In the army he was alone only on night guard duty, when he would experiment with madness by trying to see and hear things; sometimes he thought he had succeeded and that if he could repeat the effect in daylight he could get out of the army; in daylight, however, he always felt sane. On one weekend pass he so yearned to be alone that he took a hotel room and from Friday night to Monday morning had his meals sent up, spent hours in the bath, and made no phone calls. He often daydreamed that after the war he would build a square, soundproof, concrete house on a deserted stretch of beach; it would have a roof of glass bricks and no windows; only his girl friend would be admitted, and she not always. Actually after the war he married, and he and his wife moved into a small apartment. He enjoyed his wife's company except in sleep. Occasionally when his wife had risen and gone off to work he would call in sick to his office and spend the morning in bed alone. When his marriage broke up, a sixty-year-old Polish friend, a man with an accent and a lisp, told him, "Never get divorthed. If you divorth you will remarry. It followth, the night the day. You are theparated? Thtay theparated, it ith the ideal condition." "Suppose my wife gets divorced," he said. "Then lie. I have been theparated thirty yearth. I would not think of getting divorthed." "Is that really true?" he asked the friend. "That ith my thtory." At another time the friend said, "Never let a woman thtay over. I did onthe, and it took me three month to get rid of her. I had to buy her a plane ticket to Europe." When he fell in love he took a large apartment with the woman. If she was in another room he went there once an hour to touch her. Despite their troubles it was a great pleasure to sleep in the same bed with her. Even on sweaty summer nights they tucked themselves back to front, front to back, or pressed against one another back to back. Near the end of the relationship he will be surprised to hear her complain that he had never left her alone: he had thought that she liked these attentions. He will have a problem maintaining an interest in solitary activities: he will plan a leisurely, newsy letter to a friend, say, then stop midway and phone the friend instead. For a short period he will donate time to a hospital, chatting with patients who have no visitors. Nurses and sometimes a doctor will tell him how much his visits mean to patients. Occasionally he will see jealousy in a patient that he is well and will outlive the patient. He will often wonder how much life there is left to him and think that if he knew exactly he would be able to act in a way more satisfying to himself. He will also consider what he would do if he had his life to live over: certainly he would marry a woman with whom he had more in common, and yet that would mean his children would not exist; certainly he would not spend so much time on the solitary act of writing, and yet nothing that he might have done instead will occur to him.

DAYS IN THE CITY broke into parts. When his mother woke him he asked to sleep another five minutes and returned to his dream or began a new one. After she woke him again, it took fifteen minutes to wash, dress, and eat breakfast; ten minutes to walk to school, through the garden, breaking off a boxwood leaf to chew, down slate steps to the street, past the tennis courts/ice-skating rink, the dented painted-iron single-car garages, the colored people's apartment house, the school playing field, to the school-and-church building. If he was early he could stand outside and talk. The rule was to be in the classroom by nine o'clock, where he would pledge allegiance to the flag, say prayers, un-pack books, arrange pencils, pen, eraser, ruler. Then there followed an hour of teaching; and a twenty-minute recess, during which the boys played touch football and the girls jumped rope or talked. Sometimes he bought penny candy through the iron fence from an old man on the street. Then another hour or so of teaching and dismissal at noon. He walked home, buying a newspaper, had lunch on the living-room floor, read the funnies, and listened to a radio serial set in a general store. By one he was back in class for two more hours of teaching, less fifteen minutes if everyone had behaved. He was home and changed and out on the street with his friends by three-fifteen and played till a quarter to six. Dinner went from six to seven, during which he, his mother, father, and brother talked about the day. He listened to the radio from seven to seven-thirty; did homework, or nothing, in his room till nine; listened to more radio with his parents. Then pajamas, teeth, pee, and bed. Saturdays and Sundays were made of larger, odd-shaped parts. In high school there was more schoolwork and homework than in grammar school; and what had been weekday playtime was now taken up with the drama and debating societies, the school literary magazine and newspaper. On one Christmas vacation he worked for the post office, as high school boys did; he was bored by delivering packages from a truck for eight hours and was surprised at how long the time seemed. He was tired at day's end and went to sleep right after supper. A month later for the week's work he received a check for eighteen dollars and change, which he spent on a grand date with his girl friend. In college there was less schoolwork and more homework than in high school; the afternoon and evening were never long enough to do the reading, and sometimes he stayed up all night to finish his assignments: he finished *The Republic* and *On the Nature of Things* at dawn and was so excited by the experiences he could not sleep in the few hours left before classes. In the army he and his friends sometimes stayed up all night, drinking near beer, talking, and playing cards— they were pleased to deny the army fresh bodies in the morning. What was most surprising about army life was that nothing he was told to do was for himself: it was the opposite of school. After he was discharged schoolwork seemed a luxury, also unimportant. What he wanted was to get a job and be married: having his own money, wife, and home would be his true life. After two years he had an insight, which he told to his wife: "I treat you better than I treat anyone else, you treat me worse," by which he meant that she was the most important person in his life and that she, being cowardly in her dealings with relatives, friends, and even storekeepers, saved her bad humor for him. He took to sleeping when she was awake and staying up after she had gone to bed, when he would drink, read, and write fiction or letters to friends. Raising children was so hard that they put away their differences for a few years, but when they had energy again the problems were worse. Near the end of the marriage they met mainly at dinner, and otherwise kept out of one another's way. After he left home, time seemed wasted except when he was working or writing. He drank a lot, which made time pass meaninglessly; sometimes listening to music or reading (well-written ephemera particularly) settled his mind like iron filings on a paper over a magnet. When he fell in love time with the beloved was worth more than time without her; however, when the woman became discontented her complaints destroyed his joy at her presence. He will put off breaking with her for several years by going back to his old psychiatrist. Living alone will not be so bad as it had been, nor will sex have such a hold on him. As he grows older without serious illness he occasionally will be grateful that he escaped early destruction and midway disillusion. Near the end of his life he will be able to do whatever he wants with his time, civilization and nature having lost interest in him.

HE DIDN'T STOP sucking his thumb until he was eleven. For a long time his parents had been after him to give up the habit, but it was too great a source of consolation. His mother asked the help of the family doctor, a self-satisfied and all-knowing man who could tell a patient's condition from stools ("To see the world in a grain of sand," the doctor would say). The doctor advised covering the thumbs with adhesive tape; later, painting them with iodine; later, promising rewards. Nothing worked, although it must be said for the doctor that rewards were not tried. The thumb-sucking had forced a space between his two front teeth; and his father, projecting his own business concerns, explained how important personal appearance would be for him in the adult world. "Someone who makes a good appearance, a doorman opens the door immediately. Someone who doesn't make a good appearance, the doorman wants to know him first. The point I'm making," his father said, "is that for a good-looking person the doors fly open." Rather than give up thumb-sucking, however, he accepted the inevitability of ugliness and secretly planned to compensate by dressing splendidly (his father also often commented on the importance of clothes). As his twelfth Christmas approached, in the middle of the depression, he went to his father and promised to quit thumb-sucking if he could have as a present the same kind of camera his brother had bought for himself with saved money. His father agreed, recognizing that finally he wanted something more than thumb-sucking. He kept the bargain but shortly afterward started smoking cigarettes on the sly with friends. This sometimes gave him an erection. He felt that the association of naughtiness with smoking and sex accounted for the erections. (In later life an analyst reminded him that when he was very young and taken into his parents' bed at night he would sleep on his father's side and hold his father's thumb, which smelled of tobacco.) When he was fifteen he announced to his father that he had started smoking and intended to smoke at home. He didn't enjoy smoking in his father's presence and did it only in the cause of independence. He also began biting his fingernails, not so much nervously as cosmetically, and instead of spitting out the severed parts he lovingly passed them back and forth between his teeth with his tongue. Shortly after he married he went down on his wife, intending it as homage, and found that he enjoyed the taste and texture. The next girl he slept with disliked foreplay and did not allow cunnilingus. She said she was afraid he might expect her to do the same thing and she didn't want to. It was no privation at the time, but now cunnilingus is an important part of lovemaking for him: he brings a girl to the point of climax with his tongue, enters her, and either comes with her or comes later at his leisure. His taste for sucking breasts has diminished; also his taste for kissing. When he is with a woman he thinks of his mouth as auxiliary genitals. The lips of beautiful girls remain attractive to him; he likes to look at them, touch them with his fingers; but the fitting place for his mouth is in contact with their genitals. He will be drinking an Italian liqueur with a girl in bed and suggest that he pour some onto her cunt and taste it. It will sting her, so she will have to douche. When she returns to bed he will let her pour some on his penis. It will sting him too; after mock roughhouse and laughing they will fall asleep for the night. As he ages and is fearful that the next time or soon he will not be able to achieve a second erection he will reassure himself with the thought that he can always go down on a girl without end. One woman will tell him that a single fuck with affection and snuggling is all that's needed and anyone who wants more is a hog. He will act on this advice, not offer more, and never lose a woman because of sex as far as he knows. At a certain point—he will think it is when he can no longer organize his gray and thinning hair into a conventional form—women on the streets and in shops will discard him in quick looks just as he had discarded unattractive women all his life. Still he will be able to make connections at social gatherings by saying that he is interested and able, and before he gives sex up he will pride himself that he had never been impotent while sober. "My sex life," he will tell a young male interviewer at lunch after two drinks, "was troubled and full of waste but triumphant."

HE HEARD that a boy in his apartment house would soon die from a rare disease. The boy was small and pale but otherwise looked and acted well. The boy spit a lot; he wondered whether this was a symptom of the disease or a brave gesture. The boy once told him that a class-mate had exposed an erect penis under the desk in the back of the classroom. "It was so *straight!*" the boy said a number of times in reporting the incident. The boy moved away. The only child in his grammar school class to die was a dull, quiet boy named Matthew, who later was thought to have been saintly; one nun sug-gested that special requests, such as for help in remain-ing pure, might be addressed to Matthew in heaven. Some of his friends in the city had only one parent liv-ing; all the children at the beach community had both.

One day he called a city boy whose mother was dead a son of a bitch; the boy punched him on the cheek and said, "If you ever insult my mother again I'll kill you." Many grandparents died, and not much was made of it. After one boy's grandmother died and was laid out in the living room the boy told him he had felt her breasts when no one was looking. His father took him every Sunday to visit his grandmother, who lived with two aunts and an uncle. The grandmother was bedridden and had straight white hair, which one of the aunts regularly cut. When the grandmother died she was displayed in a funeral parlor; visitors were invited to kneel in front of the body and pray. An aunt beckoned him forward; he shook his head; she tried to push him from behind; he became rigid, and only a look from his father made her stop. One evening after a phone call his father told his mother that one of the father's brothers had died. "Heart?" his mother said; "Heart," his father said; and they both nodded. Nine of his original high school class of ninety died in the war. Afterward a Jesuit explained the percentage in this way: the boys had been Catholic, therefore idealistic; they had gone into the service in 1943, when the safe jobs were filled; they had been eighteen or nineteen, too young for special training, which would have delayed combat. When his father died his own doctor watched him closely, explaining that sons sometimes took the deaths of their fathers hard, developing irreversible high blood pressure. Nothing happened immediately, but a year later he became certain that he would die at any moment from a heart attack. He went to bed for two weeks, resenting that his daughters, who were seven and four at the time, would survive him. Later, when he told this to a psychiatrist, the psychiatrist pointed out that most people would have been upset at the thought of not being survived by their children. He took this for a rebuke, and the psychiatrist tried to recall the remark. When he learned on the subway, from a headline in a newspaper held by a weeping black woman, that Kennedy had been shot, for an instant he was glad, although he was an admirer of Kennedy: he had stayed up late many nights to see TV reruns of the press conferences, lifting his beer can or snapping his fingers at Kennedy's wit. There have been no natural deaths among his close friends, although he hears of the deaths of friends from the past, and friends tell him about the deaths of their friends. One such report concerned a man his age who had died from throat cancer. A month later he felt an obstruction in his throat, which he could neither swallow nor clear by hawking. For months he talked about it with a psychiatrist, who refused to answer hypothetical questions about cancer and instead kept urging him to go to a specialist for a diagnosis. Only after he was sure he was dying and had nothing to lose did he go. The doctor examined him, said he was all right, and suggested that when he felt uncomfortable he suck on a piece of hard candy. He now plays games with newspaper obituaries, picking one at random and saying, "I will die at the age this person has died at." If the age is less than his, "I've outlived the prediction; it's false." If the age is much greater he computes the difference and says, "In the meantime anything can happen." If the age is a little greater he reads the obituary for special background details: "He was a striver, now he's paid for it," or "Theatrical people lead desperate lives, and this one sounds queer." As he gets older he will sometimes try to inquire into his deepest wishes, hoping to find a weariness with life that would make death less fearsome, but can't.